Leif R. Montin

get Outta Town!™
MONTREAL

52 Fun Things to Do within Easy Reach of Montreal

NO FIXED ADDRESS PUBLICATIONS

Get Outta Town! Montreal
52 Fun Things to Do within Easy Reach of Montreal
1st edition
1st printing Sept '97
2nd printing April '98

Published by
No Fixed Address Publications, P.O. Box 65, NDG Station, Montreal, Quebec,
H4A 3P4, Canada
e-mail: nfa@cam.org

Writing: Leif R. Montin
Editing: Karin Montin
Maps: Kate McDonnell
Design and Layout: Irma Mazzonna and Caroline Villaret
Additional Icons: John Custy
Photos: Leif R. Montin / No Fixed Address Publications (except where indicated)
Photo of the Author: Owen Egan

Cover Photos (top to bottom):
Centre Educatif et Forestier des Laurentides;
La Montagne Coupée (photo: La Montagne Coupée);
Cooper Marsh;
Gatineau Park (photo: Parks Canada).

Distribution
Hushion House, 36 Northline Road, Toronto, Ontario, M4B 3E2, Canada
Tel: (416) 285-6100 Fax: (416) 285-1777

Distribution (French version)
J.D.M. Géo Distribution Inc., 5790 Donahue, St-Laurent, Québec, H4S 1C1 Canada
Tel: (514) 956-8505 Fax: (514) 956-9398

Canadian Cataloguing in Publication Data

Montin, Leif R., 1963-
    Get Outta Town!, Montreal : 52 fun things to do within easy reach of Montreal

Includes index.
ISBN 0-9681732-0-9

    1. Quebec (Province)—Guidebooks. 2. Montréal Region (Quebec)—Guidebooks. I. Title.

FC2917.5.M65 1997   917.1404'4   C97-900765-8   F1052.M65 1997

© *Copyright 1997 No Fixed Address Publications*
All rights reserved. No part of this work may be reproduced or copied in any form or by any means—graphic, electronic, or mechanical, including photocopying, recording, taping, Internet, or information storage and retrieval systems—without the written permission of the publisher and author.

Printed in Canada

To my mother, who encouraged us to travel, and still leads the way.

Special thanks to my sister Karin, whose hard work and astute editing made the book understandable. Thanks also to Nancy, Bob, and Kelle at CBC Daybreak for taking the chance; to the gang at Plan B for honing the craft, to the staff of Quebec's tourist bureaus for a wealth of information and ideas, and to all the people, too numerous to mention, who opened their doors to me in this beautiful province of ours. And many thanks to Paul Waters, who got me started.

Table of Contents

Table of Symbols	6
Welcome	7

OUTAOUAIS

Introduction	8
Map	10
Omega Park	12
Dancing with Deer in Duhamel	14
Sandy Beaches of the Outaouais	16
Gliding with the Montreal Soaring Council	18
Winter Activities in Gatineau Park	20

LAURENTIANS

Introduction	22
Map	24
Strolling Around the Parc Régional Rivière du Nord (Wilson Falls)	26
Riverside Hikes in Doncaster Park	28
Les Jardins de Rocailles (Rock Garden)	30
Mille et Un Pots (1001 Pots)	32
Hôtel l'Estérel, Montreal's Winter Mecca	34
Hiking at the Centre Touristique et Éducatif des Laurentides	36
Jovi-Foire (Summertime Fair)	38
Hiking and Picnicking in Parc Mont Tremblant (Pimbina Section)	40

LANAUDIÈRE

Introduction	42
Map	44
Parc de Chutes Dorwin (Dorwin Falls)	46
Swimming at the Rawdon Rapids and Rawdon Municipal Beach	48
Earle Moore's Canadiana Village	50
La Montagne Coupée	52
Musée Louis-Cyr (Strongman Louis Cyr Museum)	54
Waterfalls at Parc Régional des Chutes Monte à Peine et des Dalles	56
Hiking in Parc Régional des Sept Chutes	58

EASTERN TOWNSHIPS

Introduction	60
Map	62
Missisquoi Historical Society Museum	64
Wine Tour of the Eastern Townships	66
The Living Museum of Llamas (Llamadu)	68
Brome County Fair	70

Brome County Historical Society Museum 72
Gregorian Chanting at St Benoît du Lac Abbey 74
Circuit des Arts Memphrémagog (Art Tour) 76

MONTREAL, LAVAL, AND THE SOUTH SHORE
Introduction 78
Map 80
Tilting at Windmills at Pointe du Moulin 82
Year-Round Beauty at the Morgan Arboretum 84
Caribou and Timber Wolves at the Ecomuseum 86
MUC Nature Parks — West Island 88
To Infinity and Beyond at the Cosmodome 90
Four-Season, All Weather Fun at the Laval Nature Centre 92
MUC Nature Parks — East End 94
Canadian Railway Museum 96
Marsil Museum of Clothing, Textile, and Fibre 98

MONTÉRÉGIE
Introduction 100
Map 102
Cooper Marsh Conservation Area 104
Two Sandy Beaches of Montérégie 106
Sugaring off at Sucrerie de la Montagne 108
Coteau du Lac National Historic Site 110
Indian Powwows: Kahnawake and Kanesatake 112
Winter Activities at the Centre Plein Air Les Forestiers 114
"Intermiel" Bee Farm 116
Exotarium (Reptile Vivarium) 118
Pointe du Buisson Archaeological Dig 120
Électrium 122
Winter Activities at the Centre de Conservation
de la Nature Mont St Hilaire 124
Fort Chambly and Fort Lennox National Historic Sites 126
George H. Montgomery Bird Sanctuary 128

COEUR DU QUÉBEC
Introduction 130
Map 132
Waterfalls at Parc des Chutes St Ursule 134
Snow Geese Staging Grounds 136
St Tite Western Festival 138

INDEX 140

Table of Symbols

 Birdwatching

 Canoeing

 Cross Country Skiing

 Cycling/Mountain Biking

 Dogs Wecome

 Farm Animals

 Fishing

 Free Admission

 Gift shop/Boutique

 Hiking/Walking

 Historic Site

 Horseback Riding

 In-Line Skating

 Museum

 Picnicking

 Restaurant

 Rodeo

 Romantic Destination

 Science Centre

 Skating

 Something Special for Children

 Snack Bar

 Snowshoeing

 Swimming

 Tobogganing

 Trains

 Volleyball

 Waterfalls

 Waterslides

 Wheelchair Accessible

 Wildlife Observation

 Zoo

Welcome!
Now
Get Outta Town!

Montreal is such a great city, you may not often feel like leaving, even for a day! But when you do get the urge, you'll be pleased to know that there are literally hundreds of fantastic destinations perfect for the day-tripper. Country museums and fairs, riverside parks with rushing rapids, historic sites with gorgeous picnic areas, mountain trails through ancient forests ... To the west of Montreal, the river-crossed and heavily forested wilds of the Outaouais ... to the north, the rugged peaks of the Laurentians and the undiscovered hinterland of Lanaudière ... eastwards, the rolling hills of the Eastern Townships ... the majestic heartland of Coeur du Québec ... and due south, the riverine region of Montérégie.

It's all there, in the extraordinary beauty of the Quebec countryside—just a bridge or two and a short drive away.

CHOOSING A DESTINATION

Whether you want something to do with friends from out of town or with your own family, a quiet place to enjoy nature, or a lively festival where you can get lost in a crowd, you're bound to find it here.

• Wondering what to see in an unfamiliar part of the province? Trips are grouped by region for your convenience.

• Not quite sure how to spend the day? Flip the pages until something catches your eye. There is a photo of each destination, and icons in the margins show the services and activities offered in the area at a glance. Approximate driving times are given to help you plan.

• Know what you want, but not where to find it? Take a look in the index. Entries under activities like *hiking, cross-country skiing,* and *waterfalls,* as well as town names, will put you on the right track.

So what are you waiting for? Get Outta Town!

The Outaouais

Photo: Joe Singerman

In the westernmost part of Quebec, the Laurentian Mountains dip down to touch the Ottawa River, which forms the border between Quebec and Ontario. At Hull, the land turns north with the river, and the rugged granite of the Canadian Shield begins scraping through the rolling Gatineau Hills. The Quebec part of the Ottawa Valley, capped to the north by Abitibi, is known as the Outaouais. The unspoiled area is perfect for all sorts of outdoor activities. In summer, its many cottage-ringed lakes come alive with boaters and swimmers. In winter, cross-country skiers, snow-

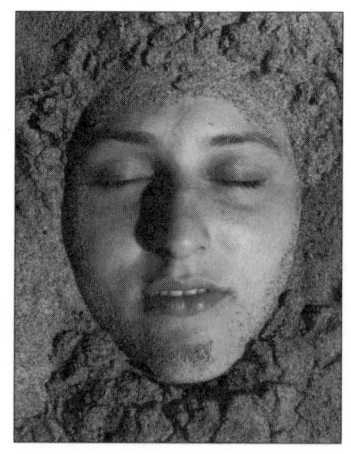

8   Get Outta Town!

mobilers, and dogsledders traverse an extensive network of trails through a countryside teeming with wildlife. This section explores a wide area of the Outaouais, from Montebello, on the Ottawa River, to the Gatineau Hills, just east of Ottawa. Here, you'll find a marvellous wildlife park open year-round, and a couple of great beaches. You'll also discover one very special town, Duhamel, where you can feed wild deer from your hand in the winter months. And if you'd like to see this rough terrain from the air, you'll be interested in the gliding club in Hawkesbury, Ont., that offers inexpensive introductory flights, most days in the warm seasons.

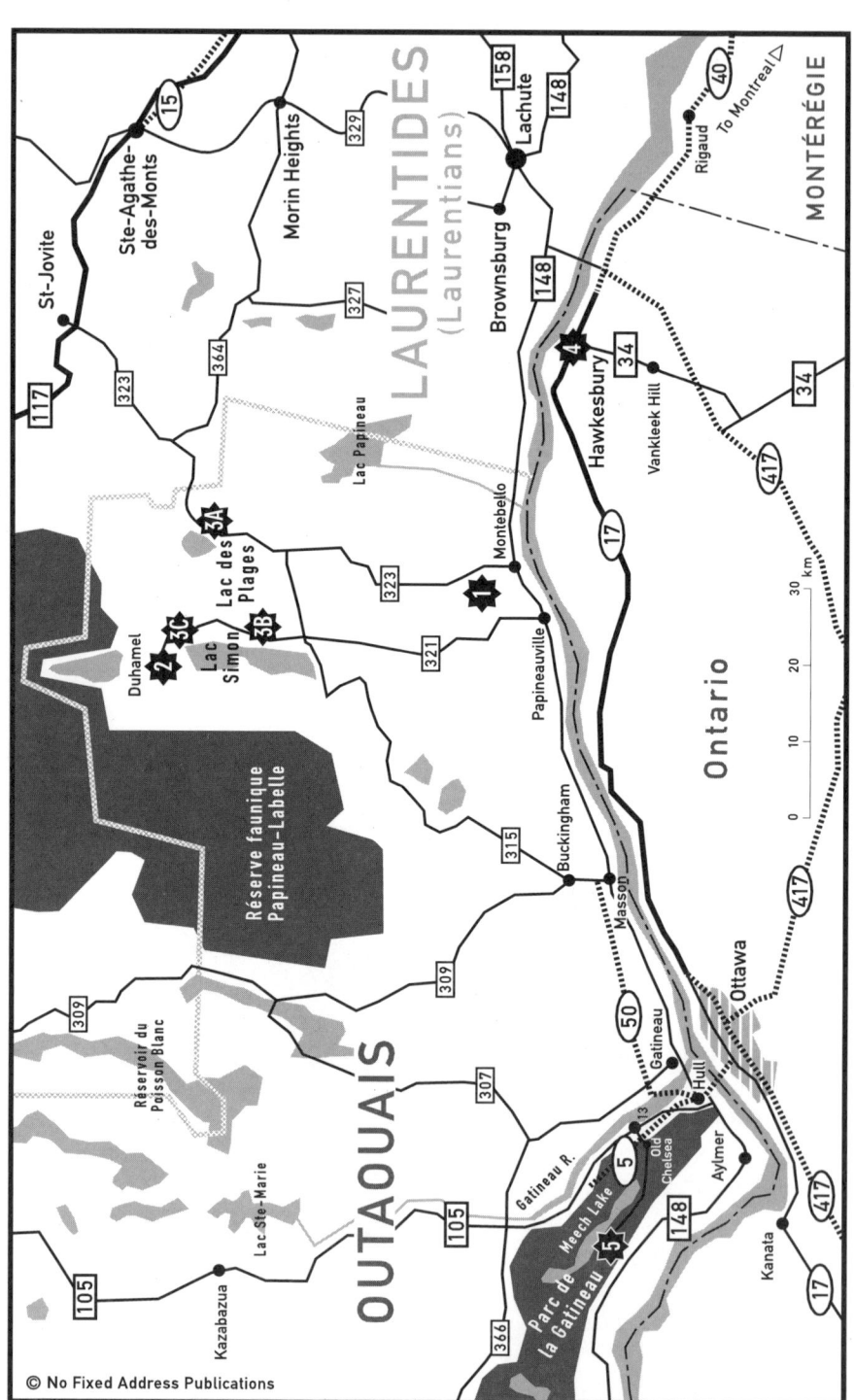

OUTAOUAIS

Trip Destinations

1 Omega Park
Near Montebello
(819) 423-5487, (819) 423-5023
p.12

2 Deer Observation
Duhamel
Restaurant: (819) 428-4242
Campground: (819) 428-3740
Festival: (819) 428-7089
p.14

3A Hôtel Mon Chez-Nous Beach
Lac des Plages
(819) 426-2186
p.16

3B Lac Simon Municipal Beach
Lac Simon
(819) 428-3905
p.16

3C Lac Simon Tourist Centre
Duhamel
(819) 428-7931
p.16

4 Montreal Soaring Council
Hawkesbury, Ont.
(613) 632-LIFT (5438), (514) 696-5889
p.18

5 Gatineau Park
Old Chelsea/The Gatineau
(819) 827-2020
p.20

Tourist Information

Outaouais Tourist Association (Hull)
(819) 778-2222

Outaouais Tourist Association
(Montebello)
(819) 423-5602

Get Outta Town! **11**

Omega Park
Near Montebello
DRIVING TIME: 1.5 HR

There are no bells and whistles or fairground rides at Omega Park. Just an old country road winding through the woods, past granite cliffs and spring-fed lakes. But this road has something extra—hundreds of animals representing over a dozen species of Canadian and European wildlife, roaming freely. The park is more than just the "alternative to the traditional visit to the zoo" described by its pamphlet. The 10-km drive through the park is like a trip through an enchanted forest.

Each species seems to prefer a different area, and the animals don't mind sharing their space with you. In fact, visitors are encouraged to take an active role in feeding them. You can buy a kilo or two of carrots at the gatehouse for a couple of dollars, or bring your own. Fruit is also a treat for the animals, but no breakfast cereal, chips, or popcorn is allowed!

The friendly, gentle creatures know that cars mean food. One elk sets up shop on a two-way stretch of road, so he can get carrots from cars going in both directions.

Roadside feeding stations provide oats, corn, hay, and salt for the deer. Four lakes are stocked with minnows to attract otters and muskrats, and park staff put corn in the water for ducks and geese. There's even a boar that can sometimes be found knee deep in the duck pond, rooting for soggy corn.

A shaded area belongs to the wild boar. Native to Europe, the boar are doing remarkably well, and dozens of young squeak excitedly each time their mothers get up to stretch their legs.

A twist in the road puts you quite suddenly on the edge of a huge grassy plain where a herd of bison are fond of grazing. Like the other animals, the bison are thriving. In summer, half a dozen calves spend their days galloping after the herd. One enormous bison has a particular liking for carrots, and personally, I don't think you've lived until you've been licked by a bison's long, rough black tongue.

The free-range nature of the park means that there are always more animals hiding out in the woods than near the road. Winter is actually a good time for a visit, since it brings most of the animals nearer to the feeding stations.

Whatever the season, your ticket is valid all day. You can drive through the park, picnic or visit Montebello, then go through again. Because the animals roam freely—only the beavers and black bears are enclosed—the living scenery is different each time.

A pamphlet identifies each of the main species inhabiting the park, including wild boar, bison, wild sheep, black bears, elk (also known as wapiti), and four kinds of deer. Better yet, tune your radio to 88.1 FM (90.1 for the French version) and a taped voice with musical interludes will give you a tour that is both educational and non-intrusive. The 45-min broadcast loop is especially designed for children.

A summertime feature is the raptor show, in which trained hawks, eagles, falcons, and even a vulture fly around and swoop down to pick up food on command. A wooden grandstand and wireless microphone make it easy to hear the bilingual commentary.

After a slow drive through the park, you can have lunch at the picnic tables or snack bar near the entrance. Children can let off steam in the playground. Two nature walks with quizzes provide another chance to get out of the car.

SEASON AND HOURS
Sunrise to sunset, all year (phone in winter for accessibility).

FEES
Summer: Adults $8; 6–14 $4.
Slightly less in winter.

INFORMATION
(819) 423-5487 or (819) 423-5023.

DIRECTIONS
Take Highway 40 (Trans-Canada) west, then branch north onto Highway 417 towards Ottawa. Take the Hawkesbury exit, then follow Highway 17 to Hawkesbury. Cross the Perly Bridge back into Quebec. Go west on Route 148, following the signs to Montebello. In Montebello, head north on Route 323.

Dancing with Deer Duhamel

DRIVING TIME: 2 HR 20 MIN

If, like most city dwellers, your contact with wild deer is limited to being tantalized by the leaping stag silhouetted on bright yellow road signs, take a trip to Duhamel. Every year the population of this small municipality north of Montebello more than quintuples when some 2,000 white-tailed deer take up residence for the winter. Duhamel is a town that will quickly, well, endear itself to you.

You'll quite likely see a deer or two in a driveway on the outskirts of town, and you'll almost certainly find half a dozen hanging out by the grocery store, but the three main viewing areas in Duhamel are Restaurant Rendez-Vous du Chevreuil, Duhamel Camping and Lodges, and the Festival du Chevreuil. (As you may have guessed, *chevreuil* means deer.)

An unassuming snack bar from the front, the Restaurant Rendez-Vous du Chevreuil has an open-ended "backyard" that is hopping, dawn to dusk, with dozens of deer. What brings them? For 10 or 15 years now, the residents of Duhamel have been laying out alfalfa, carrots, and corn, starting in October when hunting season ends. The deeper the snow, the more difficult foraging gets, and the more deer show up. And they come back for seconds. The restaurant alone goes through 500–600 bails of alfalfa a year, and over 2 tons of corn.

14 Get Outta Town!

OUTAOUAIS

Most of the deer are extremely shy. A quick arm movement, for example, sends them back to the safety of the woods. Some are a little bolder, however. One deer needed only a little coaxing to take an apple straight out of my travelling companion's mouth. You can buy apples, their favourite food, for 25¢ apiece inside, and corn from a dispenser.

If feeding a deer by hand or mouth isn't your cup of alfalfa tea, maybe you'd prefer playing among them. Duhamel Camping and Lodges clears and grooms 25 km of trails, suitable for skiing, snowshoeing, and hiking. Feeding stations keep the deer near the trails and all over the campground. You can also borrow an inner tube for the superfast toboggan run carved into a hillside. A heated shelter at the bottom gets the blood flowing again on cold days.

Another popular spot is the Festival du Chevreuil at the entrance to town, where Don McLean and Diane Filion open their backyard to visiting people and deer. They offer 12 km of well-marked and cleared skiing and hiking trails that cross an open stream on a footbridge and wind along hillsides in circular routes. This is the most natural of the areas, so you'll need a keen eye, but you can spot deer bounding through the woods or standing stock-still among the trees. Follow the arrows and you won't get lost.

Duhamel is at the crossroads of a number of snowmobile trails. Adventurers might want to rent one at the Chateau Montebello (and head north), or in St Agathe (and head west). A driver's licence is required. The trip is about 2 hr, from either centre.

SEASON AND HOURS
Sunrise to sunset Dec 1–Mar 31 (Jan and Feb are peak months). Best times dawn and dusk.

FEES
Restaurant and Festival: Free (donations accepted). Campground: Deer observation $3 per car; activities $3 per person.

INFORMATION
Outaouais Tourist Office (Montebello) (819) 423-5602;
Restaurant (819) 428-4242;
Campground (819) 428-3740;
Festival (819) 428-7089.

DIRECTIONS
Take Highway 40 (Trans-Canada) west, then branch north onto Highway 417 towards Ottawa. Take the Hawkesbury exit, then follow Highway 17 to Hawkesbury. Cross the Perly Bridge back into Quebec. Go west on Route 148, following the signs to Montebello. At Papineauville, take Route 321 north to Duhamel. For a more scenic route, take Route 148 west from Lachute.
The Festival du Chevreuil is on the south edge of town (where you enter). To get to the restaurant, turn right at the flashing sign in town and follow the road for 1 km. The campground is 1 km farther.

Sandy Beaches of the
Outaouais
North of Montebello

DRIVING TIME: 1.5-2 HR

With more than 20,000 lakes and dozens of rivers to choose from, finding a spot for a swim in the Outaouais sounds about as difficult as falling off a log. But if you want sandy beaches, supervised swimming, and all mod cons, that narrows it down a little. There are certainly beaches closer to Montreal (see the section on Montérégie), but there's nothing like a beach in the heart of cottage country for that feeling of discovery. It's hard to beat a refreshing dip and a sprawl on the sand in the rugged surroundings of the Outaouais.

Lac des Plages (Beach Lake) is about 43 km north of Montebello on Highway 323. This aptly named municipality is nestled on the shore of a beautiful lake ringed with summer cottages, motels, forests, and golden sand. While most of the waterfront is privately owned, there are two more or less public beaches on the lake. The first is the municipal beach, open only to residents and guests of local hotels and motels.

The second is opposite Hôtel Mon Chez-Nous, a charming old hotel on

16 Get Outta Town!

the north edge of town about a kilometre past the municipal beach. Run by the hotel, this is a quiet family beach with a large grassy area, sandy waterfront, and a little pier stretching out over the shallow waters of the lake. Part of the beach is set aside for hotel guests, but most of it is open to day visitors. Cheerful red and white striped changing cabins are roomy and clean. You can get snacks and drinks at the waterside patio, conveniently located outside the gate to the beach, so you don't have to pay the admission charge.

A little farther north, the municipality of **Lac Simon** has a public beach on a sheltered bay at the foot of the lake of the same name. This is a very busy little sandy beach, family oriented, with toilets, changing rooms, and supervised swimming, plus parking for 50 vehicles.

About 45 min north of Montebello, the hamlet of **Duhamel** offers a broad swath of splendid sand at the head of Lac Simon. The Centre touristique du Lac Simon (Lac Simon Tourist Centre) has it all: camping facilities, volleyball nets, sailboat and sailboard rentals, minigolf, and a snack bar, served up on 2 km of sand with a remarkable view directly south the length of the lake. A fairly steady breeze off the lake makes this a sailboarding paradise. The crowd is youthful, and there are usually a number of power boats and Sea-doos buzzing outside the limits of the supervised swimming area.

Alcohol is not allowed, but that didn't seem to stop many from sneaking in a little something. Although there are secluded areas with picnic tables suitable for family swimming and picnicking, the main beach can be rather breezy, boozy, and noisy—but, hey, that might be just what you're looking for in a beach.

SEASON AND HOURS
Summer, generally June 24–Labour Day.

FEES
Lac des Plages: Adults $3.50 ($2.50 after 2 p.m.); children $1.50. Municipality of Lac Simon: Free. Lac Simon Tourist Centre: Adults $4, children $2.

INFORMATION
Montebello Tourist Office
(819) 423-5602;
Hotel Mon Chez-Nous (819) 426-2186;
Municipality of Lac Simon
(819) 428-3905;
Lac Simon Tourist Centre (819) 428-7931.

DIRECTIONS
Take Highway 40 (Trans-Canada) west, then branch north onto Highway 417 towards Ottawa. Take the Hawkesbury exit, then follow Highway 17 to Hawkesbury. Cross the Perly Bridge back into Quebec. Go west on Route 148, following the signs to Montebello. In Montebello, head north on Route 323.

Gliding with the Montreal Soaring Council
Hawkesbury, Ont.
DRIVING TIME: 1 HR

T he Montreal Soaring Council is an offshoot of the McGill Soaring Club that in the '30s—incredible as it seems—took off from downtown Fletcher's Field (the greenspace divided by Park Ave). Its new incarnation is a volunteer-run, non-profit organization with its own airfield, clubhouse, power planes, and gliders—even a dog named Windsock. But it's always looking for new enthusiasts, and by way of encouragement, it offers inexpensive and thrilling introductory flights to potential members on weekends all season long.

Since flights are arranged on first-come, first-served basis, you might want to get there early (say 10 a.m.). You can help unpack the hangar, where a dozen gliders are stacked like a Chinese puzzle. The club has a number of models, from slower trainers to wasp-shaped high-performance planes that look like champagne flutes with 20-m wings.

What all share is an incredible grace and stability in the air. If you take your hands and feet off the controls, a glider will continue to sail in a straight line, losing altitude according to its glide ratio (forward travel to horizontal drop). Glide ratios range from 29:1 for trainers to 40:1 for high-performance planes. In comparison, a 747 jumbo jet has a brick-like glide ratio of 17:1.

Taking off is very exciting. A power plane tows your glider up into the sky. During this part of the flight, the pilot must keep the nose of the glider just below the tail of the tow-plane, anticipate each updraft, and react accordingly. It's like midair water-skiing.

Once you drop the towline, gliding is a game of looking for thermals, the updrafts that lift you to new heights and prolong your flight. The catch is that thermals are invisible, and the pilot must take his or her cues from nature—clouds or birds, mainly. A good pilot can stay up for hours, and travel hundreds of kilometres. My pilot and I reached an altitude of 1,400 m—pretty darn high, but a little short of the stratospheric world record of 18,000 m!

When you find an updraft, you enter a steeply banked turn to remain within it. From your position as passenger, it appears as if the downward wing is pinned down and the plane is spinning like a mobile. Oddly enough, from the ground it looks as if you are describing elongated circles a few hundred metres in diameter.

Your flight will most likely take you up and over Hawkesbury, the gentle Ottawa River, and the rapids of the Rouge River. Keep your eyes peeled for white-water rafters and the bungee-jumping tower. Thrill seekers might convince their pilots to demonstrate "dolphining," for the roller-coaster ride of a lifetime.

Soaring high above the earth ... riding upwards in widening spirals ... swooping down like an eagle ... the only sound the wind rushing across your wings. If you get dizzy in a rocking chair, you might not be cut out for gliding. Otherwise, the next time you see fluffy white clouds above, head out to Hawkesbury for a ride in the sky with a friendly gang, above some fantastic scenery.

SEASON AND HOURS
Every fine weekend, late April–late Oct.
Often on weekdays, June–Aug (call ahead).
Arrive for 10 a.m.; flying starts at noon.

FEES
$50 for introductory flight lasting a maximum of 30 min. Subsequent flights (same day) are somewhat cheaper. Must be 14 or over.

INFORMATION
(514) 696-5889.
(613) 632-LIFT (5438).

DIRECTIONS
Take Highway 40 (Trans-Canada) west, then branch north onto Highway 417 towards Ottawa. Take the Hawkesbury exit, then follow Highway 17 north. Another 2–3 km past the last exit to Hawkesbury, turn right at the T-junction onto Prescott-Russel Road 4. Follow the signs to the Montreal Soaring Council, a few kilometres along on the right-hand side.

Winter Activities in Gatineau Park
The Gatineau

DRIVING TIME: 2 HR 20 MIN

Nestled between the Ottawa River to the west and the Gatineau River Valley a few dozen kilometres to the east, the Gatineau Hills rise up suddenly, rocky and rolling. Densely forested and dotted with granite-edged lakes, this rugged landscape marks the southern limits of the Canadian Shield. A huge portion (356 km²) of this scenic region is a national park and has become a favourite summer and autumn destination for campers from Quebec and Ontario. In winter, Gatineau Park's accessibility and excellent facilities make it popular with skiers, snowshoers, and hikers alike.

All good stays begin at the visitor's centre, a cosy country house on Meech Lake Rd as you approach from Ottawa. The friendly, well-informed bilingual staff are pleased to help. Complimentary hot drinks are served, and push buttons galore will occupy little ones while you sort out maps and passes. Then it's back in the car to head for the parking lot near the trail you want to explore.

Snowshoers can choose from three maintained trails. The Brook Trail is just over 1 km and takes a circular route from the visitor's centre. The Pond Trail is shorter, but more challenging.

Most popular is the 3 km Larriault Trail. It begins at the Mackenzie King Estate, the late prime minister's summer home. (It was under Mackenzie

20 Get Outta Town!

King that the park was formed, and upon his death he bequeathed his land to the people of Canada.)

An easy walk with some hills, the Larriault Trail leads into the woods via Mackenzie King's collection of Romanesque ruins. Ambling gently up to the edge of the Eardley Escarpment, this trail affords several marvellous views of the farmland of the Ottawa Valley and the Ottawa River.

Gatineau Park also offers 15 km of groomed hiking trails. Or try your hand at kicksledding: One person sits while another pushes the "dogless dogsled" from behind, jumping onto the runners for downhill runs.

In winter, the park is best known for almost 200 km of beautifully groomed and carefully signposted cross-country ski trails. From the wide and mainly flat Parkway (closed to vehicles in winter) ideal for novices and families, to steep, winding pitches that will give pause to the most reckless downhillers, there are trails for everyone. There are 73 km for skate-skiers, and ungroomed trails as well.

Seven heated cabins with crackling wood fires and splendid views are ideal places to eat lunch or warm up during the day.

For an unforgettable experience, spend a night or two in one of five lodges in the heart of the park. Like the trails, accommodations range from the primitive (though heated) prospector-style tents on Taylor Lake to the relative luxury of the electric heating and full kitchens of the Brown Lake lodge. All provide comfortable bunks and shared community-style facilities. Some have telephones. Reservations are required.

You can rent snowshoes, kicksleds, or baby gliders at the visitor's centre. Skis must be rented outside the park. Dogs are permitted on leashes, but not overnight.

SEASON AND HOURS
Park: All day, every day, year round.
Visitor's centre: 9:30 a.m.–4:30 p.m. weekdays and 9 a.m.–5 p.m. weekends.

FEES
Trail fees: Adults $7, youth 12–17 $4.50, under 12 free; free on Thursdays.
Hut rental: $15–$35 per night.

INFORMATION
(819) 827-2020.

DIRECTIONS
Take Highway 20 or 40 (Trans-Canada) west, then branch north onto Highway 417 to Ottawa. Take the Queensway into Ottawa, and get off at the Nicholas St/ Mann Ave exit. Follow King Edward St through Hull, continuing on Highway 5 north. Do not follow the signs to Gatineau; these lead to the town, not the park. At exit 13 (Old Chelsea/Tenaga), follow the signs to the visitor's centre on Meech Lake Rd. The park is 20 min from downtown Ottawa.

Laurentians

It would be hard to list all the festivals, special events, and activities that await you directly north of Montreal in Quebec's most famous mountains. Unspoiled nature is around every corner, but there is no shortage of cultural attractions, either. Whatever the season, there will be something to suit your fancy.

Whether you like rugged hiking or easy picnicking, you'll enjoy the waterfalls and unblemished views in the Pimbina section of Mont Tremblant Provincial Park. For comfortable trails and spectacular vistas, head to the Centre Touristique et Éducatif des Laurentides

near St Agathe. (One of the views is presented on the cover.) Doncaster Park, on the outskirts of Mont Rolland, is often overlooked. Its riverside trails are easily accessible in summer, but it is great any time of year. Even closer to home is the Parc Régional Rivière du Nord (Wilson Falls), a mere 30 min from the city. It's another beauty, with seething rapids racing through it, in the warmer seasons.

This section also covers two festivals: the Jovi-Foire, St Jovite's lively summertime fair, and Mille et Un Pots, a celebration of hand-crafted ceramics in the very pretty town of Val David.

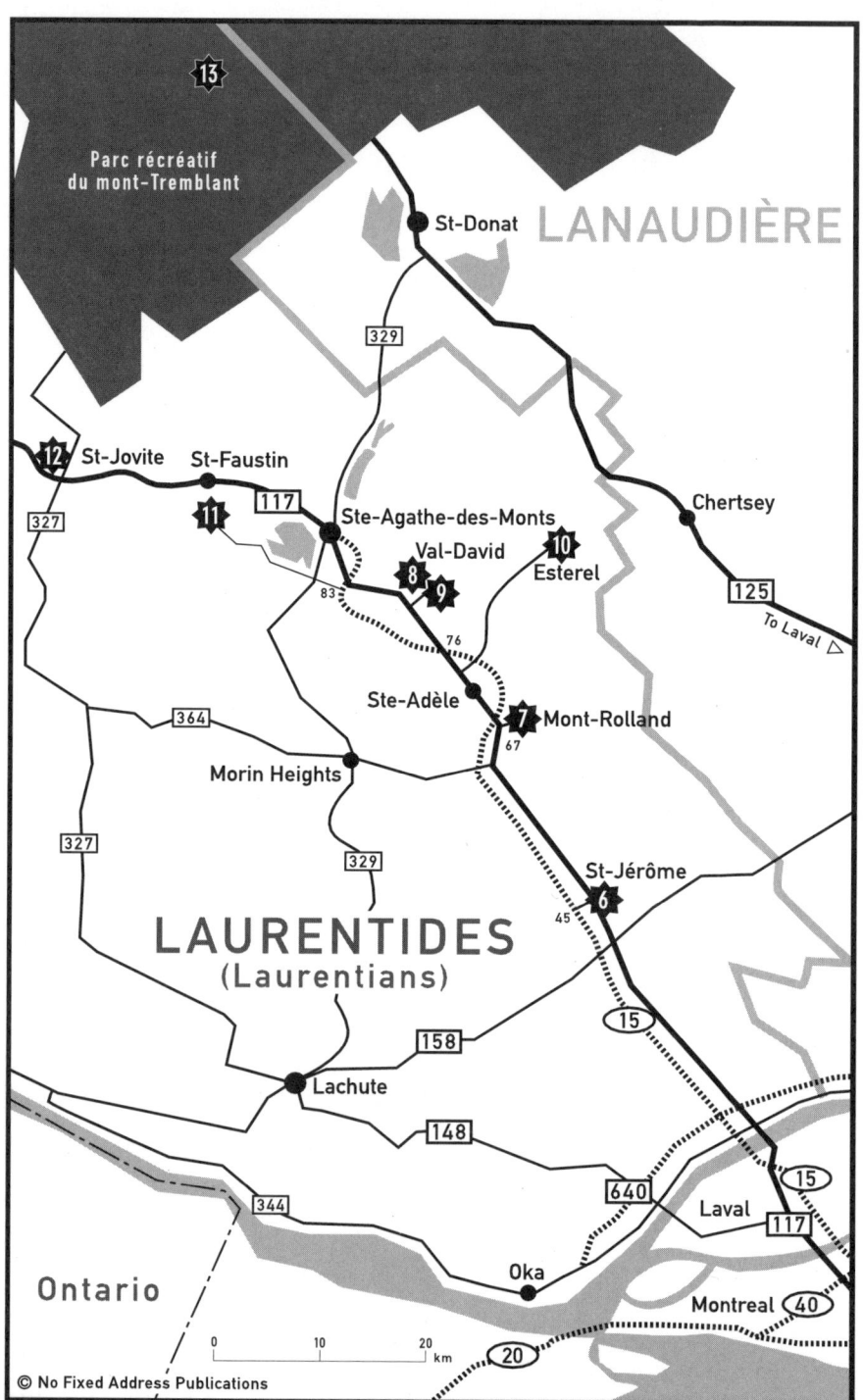

LAURENTIANS

Trip Destinations

6 Parc Régional Rivière du Nord
(Wilson Falls)
St Jérôme
(514) 431-1676
p.26

7 Doncaster Park
Mont Rolland
(514) 229-6233
p.28

8 Les Jardins de Rocailles
(Rock Garden)
Val David
(819) 322-6193
p.30

9 Mille et Un Pots (1001 Pots)
Val David
(819) 322-6868
p.32

10 Hôtel l'Estérel
Estérel
(514) 228-2571, (800) 363-8224
p.34

11 Centre Touristique et Éducatif
des Laurentides
Near St Agathe/St Faustin
(819) 326-1606
p.36

12 Jovi-Faire (Summertime fair)
St Jovite
(819) 425-8441
p.38

13 Parc Mont Tremblant
(Pimbina Section)
St Donat
Visitor's Centre: (819) 424-2964
Campground: (819) 424-7012
p.40

Tourist Information

Laurentian Tourist Association
(514) 436-8532

St Agathe Tourist Bureau
(819) 326-0457

St Jovite Tourist Bureau
(819) 425-3300

Val David Tourist Bureau
(819) 322-1515

Strolling Around the Parc Régional
Rivière du Nord
(Wilson Falls)
St Jérôme

DRIVING TIME: 30 MIN

Most people heading north barely slow down at St Jérôme. They take the left fork, following the wide curve that to many simply means the fastest route to cottage country. Those in less of a hurry often opt for the smaller Route 117 on the right. Few realize that between these two choices there lies a third: the Parc Régional Rivière du Nord, also known as Wilson Falls, nestled snugly in the vee of the two highways. This is a precious gem of a park where you can stroll, bike, or hike through the mixed forest of the lower Laurentians, or picnic beside an energetic river with rapids sparkling in the sunlight. It's hard to imagine a park of such beauty seemingly hemmed in on all sides by highways, and a scant 30-min drive from Montreal, but there it is.

Initially the park feels rather like Montreal's own Mount Royal: the paths are wide and well maintained, and the cyclists and strollers seem cut from a very urban cloth. But unlike those on Mount Royal, the footpaths and bike paths are separate, so there's no risk of being run down by a mad cyclist.

A pleasant trail leads from behind the visitor's centre down to the river, where a beautifully maintained large wooden footbridge leads into the heart

26 Get Outta Town!

of the park. Most paths follow the river, but no matter which you take, you will seldom be far from the scent of spruce, or out of earshot of the rapids, and only occasionally will you hear the highway, despite its nearness.

One of the nicest trails leads through a deeply wooded area offering occasional glimpses of the river. A short walk brings you to a stand of enormous and ancient pine trees under which are a number of picnic tables, covered against inclement weather. Here you will also find a three-sided wooden hut, especially designed for skiers.

Wilson Falls themselves are a low but attractive splash of water. They are named after the family that owned the pulp and paper mill that ran from 1881 to 1950. Kids will love clambering across the ruins of the mill, which include the remnants of a hydro-power turbine sluice about 2 m in diameter. A great concrete dam upriver is another feature of the park.

A little higher up, the trail opens onto the granite of the river. There's no better place for sunbathing than on the large, flat riverine rocks at the head of the park. In autumn, the leaves changing on the far shore, the rapids, and the exposed granite make for some excellent photographs.

The park offers a number of self-guided family adventures. There's the Sentier des Mille Sensations (Trail of a Thousand Senses), where you follow a rope through the woods blindfolded for an intimate experience of the Laurentian forest. The park offers do-it-yourself treasure hunts for ages 7 and up, as well as self-taught family orienteering for ages 10 and up, with compass supplied in return for a small deposit. In addition, you can rent a canoe for an outing on a calm stretch of the river.

In winter there are 24 km of groomed cross-country ski trails. Or, you can head off the beaten track on snowshoes. Each year, the park builds a giant ice slide just behind the visitor's centre. A wood stove in the three-sided log cabin mentioned earlier provides welcome warmth.

SEASON AND HOURS
Sunrise to sunset (9 a.m.–5 p.m. in winter), every day.

FEES
$3 per carload.

INFORMATION
(514) 431-1676.

DIRECTIONS
Take Highway 15 (Laurentian Autoroute) north to exit 45 (Montée St Thérèse), the right-hand fork onto Route 117. Immediately turn left across Route 117 on the overpass, and follow Boulevard International in the direction of St Agathe. You will seem to be returning to the highway. The entrance to the park is about 200 m along, on the right.

Riverside Hikes in Doncaster Park
Mont Rolland

DRIVING TIME: 1 HR 20 MIN

Mont Rolland is an unspoiled little Laurentian town just north of St Sauveur that seems to have escaped the commercial blight that has affected other areas. A few kilometres northeast of the village centre, on the banks of the sometimes calm, sometimes frothing Doncaster River, is the equally unspoiled Doncaster Park. This diamond in the rough makes a great day-trip destination for strolling and hiking, and in winter, skiing, far from the madding crowd.

From the gravel parking lot, a functional metal footbridge leads across

28 Get Outta Town!

the river to a broad, level central path that runs east-west the length of the park. Trail maps should be available, but there's no need to worry about getting lost if they aren't. A large map at the entrance will help you get oriented, and all the park's 13 km of trails loop off and return to the central path. Some wander up the nearby hillside; others follow the banks of the moody but lovely river. The central pathway heads west to meet the Riviere du Nord.

One of the best trails is the Chemin des Cascades (Rapids Trail). This rather rugged, rocky trail leads through typical Laurentian forest to the river's edge, and alongside some terrific rapids. They are really spectacular during the spring run-off or after a heavy rain. Amusing "no nudity" signs are reminders of the time, not so long ago, when the park was well known for its nudism.

In winter, many of the park's trails are snowmobile-groomed for cross-country skiing and there are heated shelters. Dry toilets are open all year round.

Doncaster Park is the only park that joins up with Le P'tit Train du Nord, the right of way of an abandoned railway that is now a linear park extending from St Jerome to Mont Laurier, 200 km to the north. It is also one of the few parks in Quebec where dogs are welcome.

SEASON AND HOURS
Sunrise to sunset, every day.
FEES
Free.
INFORMATION
(514) 229-6233.
DIRECTIONS
Take Highway 15 (Laurentian Autoroute) north to exit 67 (Mont Rolland). Turn right to cross over the highway and descend into the village. From the village centre (at the P'tit Train du Nord park), take Rolland Rd to Doncaster Rd, then follow the signs to Doncaster Park. It is exactly 5.25 km from the village centre.

Les Jardins de Rocailles
(Rock Garden) Val David

DRIVING TIME: 1 HR

The area around Val David is well known for its rock-climbing. On a sunny summer weekend, you might find half a dozen groups scrambling up any of the three rocky peaks that rise above this small Laurentian community. But those who like their rocks a little more horizontal will find Val David has something for them, as well.

The Jardins de Rocailles is an English-style country rock garden on the edge of picturesque Lac Sapinière (Fir Lake). This intimate little garden packs over 250 colourful varieties of flowering plants—including over 30 varieties of day lilies—into less than half a hectare.

The garden began in 1975, when trees were cut down and rocks removed to widen the road. As Claude Savard and Jeannine Parent tidied up, one thing led to another, and they have been lovingly tending the garden since then. One of the two greets every guest, and is pleased to give you a personal tour of the grounds, which have been open to the public since 1995.

The garden is planted mainly with perennials (flowers that bloom every year and can survive the winter unprotected), but a handful of annuals (flowers that live and die in one season) brighten up newly planted areas. Rich and fleshy red begonias, in full bloom in June, are the only plants that must be taken inside for the winter. Because the season is two weeks behind Montreal's, flowers that have come and gone in the city are often at their peak in Val David.

Double-flowered impatiens is an interesting plant that looks much like a small rosebush. The large, lupine-like foxglove prompted English essayist John Ruskin to write that they were the very image of human life—with long stems sporting flowers in all stages of bud, bloom, and decay. The leaves of the foxglove (whose scientific name is *Digitalis*) are used to make heart medicine.

The grounds also boast a remarkable statue garden, displaying the abstract yet meditative works of local sculptor Alain-Marie Tremblay. A small wall of water is central to the statue garden. Partially hidden by the flowing water are tiles of dancing figures, consciously reminiscent of the erotic temple statuary of Khajuraho, India. But there is a Canadian influence, too. Tiles near the base of the wall feature beavers scurrying about.

A licensed dining room on the grounds offers everything from a cup of coffee to a full à la carte meal. An inexpensive all-you-can-eat buffet of fare for the health-conscious is served Sundays from 10 a.m. until 2 p.m. The room is hung with floral-inspired works by local artists.

The village of Val David also has plenty to offer. Picnickers can spread their blankets in the Parc des Amoureux (Lovers' Park), a mere stone's throw from the garden. The park is quiet and shady, and is cooled by the Rivière du Nord that flows through it.

If you'd like to get out on the river, you can rent kayaks and canoes in Val David. You might want to bring your bicycle or rent one in town, and spend part of the day exploring the P'tit Train du Nord, the old railway right of way that is now a bicycle and hiking path. It runs from St Jerome to Mont Laurier, 200 km to the north.

SEASON AND HOURS
9 a.m–10 p.m., 15 June–Labour Day.

FEES
Adults $2.50; children free; no charge if dining. Supplemental fees for Saturday afternoon concerts (4 p.m.).

INFORMATION
(819) 322-6193.

DIRECTIONS
Take Highway 15 (Laurentian Autoroute) north to exit 76 (Val David/Val Morin). Follow Route 117 a short distance north to Val David. Follow Rue de l'Église through the town, then turn right on De la Sapinière, just past the bicycle path. Turn left on Lavoie. The Jardins de Rocailles is on the right-hand side of the road. Parking is on the left.

Mille et Un Pots
(1001 Pots)
Val David
DRIVING TIME: 1 HR

There are between 250 and 300 active potters and other ceramists in Quebec, over half of them based in the Greater Montreal area. At the height of summer, a good number of these make their way north to Val David, where they display their work for almost a month. The emphasis is on the functional, but you'll find a healthy dose of sculpture, jewellery, and the purely decorative, plus some creations that can only be classified as works of art. If you're looking for hands-on experience, you'll be happy to know there are a number of workshops offered as well.

This celebration of all things ceramic began in 1989, when long-time

Val David resident Kinya Ishikawa brought together 50 artists, with 20 pieces each. (*Pot* is French ceramic-trade jargon for any piece of work.) The show has grown each year, and now counts 100 artists displaying at least 100 pieces each. So it's actually 10,001 pots, or maybe even 20,001, but the original name has stuck. And the idea is catching on—imitators have already sprung up in Honolulu, Martinique, and Bordeaux!

Though it is now the largest ceramic show on the continent, it is still a very cosy gathering. The pieces are laid out attractively on low tables arranged on the gently undulating lawn between Mr Ishikawa's house, studio, and gallery on a hill at the entrance to the village. There is absolutely no pressure to purchase. In fact, you might have a hard time finding a ceramist, as most leave their wares unattended.

While the pieces are generally grouped by artist, a wall of coffee mugs is a noteworthy exception. In addition, an indoor gallery displays artistic works of extraordinary beauty, with price tags to match. (Prices at the show range from $4 to $2,500.)

Special activities in 1996 included an attempt to establish the world record for most pots thrown in a day. Teams of four threw 1,089 pots in four hours using just one wheel—and half a ton of clay! They'll attempt the feat again in 1997, for an entry in the *Guinness Book of World Records*.

On weekends you can get your hands dirty in a number of on-site workshops such as raku. This is the Japanese technique of airless firing under leaves that results in marvellous patterns where the glazes are oxydized to different degrees. Or you could keep them clean by learning Japanese flower arranging and sushi making.

SEASON AND HOURS
10 a.m.–7 p.m., every day, Jul 27–Aug 18 in 1996 (varies). The exhibition moves to Quebec City in late Aug, and Montreal in early Sept.

FEES
Free. Charges apply for workshops.

INFORMATION
(819) 322-6868.

DIRECTIONS
Take Highway 15 (Laurentian Autoroute) north to exit 76 (Val David/Val Morin). Follow Route 117 a short distance north to Val David. Take Rue de l'Église into the town. La Galerie Val David is at 2435 Rue de L'Église.

Hôtel l'Estérel
Montreal's Winter Mecca
Estérel
DRIVING TIME: 1 HR 20 MIN

Hôtel l'Estérel is well known in summer for its golf course and marina on the edge of meandering Lake Dupuis. But a sunny winter's day can attract as many as 600 visitors, mainly families and young couples, to this year-round resort. And no wonder. In winter, Estérel is a bustling centre for snow-based recreation: everything from ice-skating to hot-air ballooning, including dogsledding, snowmobiling, horse-drawn sledding, and ice-fishing. All this in addition to some of the best cross-country skiing (and cheapest trail rates) Quebec has to offer.

The hotel boasts 85 km of trails groomed daily, 15 km especially for skate-skiers. Another 11 km are ungroomed, for a backwoods experience. All trails are extremely well marked, and a clear trail map is provided with your pass.

The golf course trails are ideal for first-timers, though most trails run through woods and over gently rolling hills. The adventurous will get a kick out of Trail 13, which hugs the lakeside hills and presents some great views.

34 Get Outta Town!

LAURENTIANS

Taken counterclockwise from the hotel, it yields a few fantastic downhill runs, without too much uphill legwork. A couple of big blue teepees with fires inside provide warmth on the busier trails. There is also a heated waxing room and a nice cafeteria overlooking the lakeside activities (outside lunches are not permitted).

Skiing veteran Bill Deskin and others are on hand for lessons. Bill really knows his stuff. I had been cross-country skiing for many years, but never really enjoyed it. After a mere 15-minute conversation, Bill had straightened out my technique, and I have loved the sport ever since. According to Bill, if you can walk one mile you can ski five, because you glide the other four.

If you're still not convinced that cross-country skiing's for you, how about ice-skating on the lake? The hotel clears and waters a snow-ringed skating rink every year. To really stretch your legs, you can skate the 6-km track to St Marguerite on nearby Lake Masson. (You drive through St Marguerite to get to Estérel.)

For a truly Canadian experience, go dogsledding with Richard Lapointe, whose good-natured dogs really love to run. You can be a musher for only 20 min or up to a full day. Overnight trips are also possible. One of his lead dogs, Blackie, was featured in the film *Agaguk*.

On weekends when the weather is good, you can try your hand at hot-air ballooning, in either a tethered balloon, or the more adventurous (and expensive) guided free flight. You can also rent a snowmobile.

The hotel organizes a special weekend (usually the first one in January) called the Kite and Ski Fest. As the name implies, there are demonstrations of winter kite-flying, plus acrobatic kite-flying on skis (snow and wind permitting). Snow golf on the lake played with golf clubs and tennis balls is a hoot! Just one hole, but it's a par 35.

SEASON AND HOURS
8 a.m –5 p.m., 7 days a week.

FEES
Trail fees: Adults $6; students $3, under 12 free.
Dogsledding: 20 min $24, half day $75, full day $140 (mid-afternoon lunch included).
Snowmobile rental: 1 hr $79, half day $148, full day $210. Marginally more for second person. Complete outfit included. Driver's licence required.

INFORMATION
(514) 228-2571 or (800) 363-8224.

DIRECTIONS
Take Highway 15 (Laurentian Autoroute) north to exit 69 (l'Estérel). From there, follow Route 370 east 15 km to Estérel. The hotel is clearly signposted from the exit.

Hiking at the Centre Touristique et Éducatif des Laurentides
Near St Agathe/St Faustin
DRIVING TIME: 1 HR 20 MIN

Once upon a time, a group of businessmen discovered Cordon Lake, the most beautiful lake in all the Laurentians. It was of a deep blue colour seldom seen this side of the Rockies. It was chiselled out of the mountains and fringed by exposed granite and lush forest. From the peak of the hill rising steeply on one edge was the most spectacular view imaginable. They bought the lake, the mountain, and the forest, and for many years kept it as a private fishing and hunting lodge. This fairy-tale scene is now open to the public. The municipality of St Faustin runs the site, which offers hillside trails and boardwalks in addition to canoeing and fishing.

All hikes begin and end at the visitor's centre, a very cosy building in traditional Laurentian architectural style. Here you'll find trail maps and staff who can help you choose a route based on the time you have and the challenge you desire. But there really is no better way to get oriented than by studying the excellent three-dimensional model of the area, with all trails clearly indicated.

While there is no snack bar or restaurant in the centre, there's always a hot pot of coffee to help you get started and a cold-drink machine to welcome you back. You can picnic at covered outdoor tables (some along the trails themselves). While parents sort themselves out, youngsters will be amply entertained by the nature exhibits, including stuffed and mounted animals, and a couple of wooden xylophones.

There are six hikes to choose from, for a total of 13 km of beautifully marked and perfectly maintained trails, of all levels of difficulty and varying lengths. All of them are circular routes with very little doubling back. Most of them are also one-way, so are seldom congested, even in the busy months.

By all measures, the best trail is the Panoramique, a 1.5-hr return trip at a leisurely pace. This trail leads up the hillside, but has wide wooden staircases up the steepest parts.

The view from the lookout at the top of the Panoramique is incredible. There you are 200 m above the deep blue Cordon Lake (already 360 m above sea level). The view sweeps westward over the thick forests and softening peaks of the Laurentians as they fade into the region of the Outaouais. Not a house, highway, or electrical pylon in sight. This is surely one of the most spectacular views in the Laurentians. (Photo enthusiasts take note: the best light is in the morning, when the sun is behind you.)

The Aquatique (2 km, 45 min) and the Riverain (1 km, 30 min) are two lovely trails leading through the woods and across Cordon Lake, where it narrows. The common entrance leads over an arched wooden bridge, then travels alongside and across lakes on a series of very wide boardwalks that wind their way along the shoreline.

The more sedentary may prefer to rent a canoe. If you're in a big gang, consider taking the 12-seat *rabaska* for a paddle. Fishing is allowed, but a valid licence is required.

Some lakeside trails are wheelchair accessible.

SEASON AND HOURS
Visitor's centre: 8:30 a.m.– 4:30 p.m., every day, May–Oct.

FEES
General $3, $2.50 per person for groups of 20, under 5 free. Canoe rental: $6 per hour, *rabaska* $15 per hour.

INFORMATION
(819) 326-1606.

DIRECTIONS
Take Highway 15 (Laurentian Autoroute) north to exit 83 (just before St Agathe). Follow Montée Alouette, Chemin du Tour du Lac, then Chemin du Lac Manitou. All of these roads lead in a straight line northwest. Finally, turn west on Chemin du Lac Caribou, following the signs for CTEL (Centre Touristique et Éducatif des Laurentides).

Jovi-Foire
(Summertime Fair)
St Jovite

DRIVING TIME: 1 HR 15 MIN

When a film company needs a specific landscape or building for a project, it often hires a local expert, called a location scout, to find it. A good scout has catalogues of photographed locations and can earn up to $500 a day, plus expenses.

A couple of summers ago, I spent a day exploring the back roads of the western Laurentians and eastern Outaouais with a location scout. At the end of the long and exhausting foray, we rattled into St Jovite and stumbled upon the delightful Jovi-Foire, St Jovite's annual combination street and music festival. We were immediately swept up in the warmth and bustle of this summertime celebration, which is family oriented by day, with plenty for grown-ups in the evening.

Almost every merchant in this pleasant tourist town gets involved in the Thursday-to-Sunday festival. A full schedule of events includes everything from clowns and jugglers to tennis workshops and magic shows. All activities take place along Rue Ouimet, the main street, and almost all are free.

Children will enjoy the minifarm petting zoo, multiperson bicycle rides through town, hay rides, a supervised climbing wall, and especially the taffy made by pouring maple syrup on snow (called *tire*, pronounced tier). There's a hamster race, in which each child cheers a particular hamster on, and races in which children run with their own dogs. A small midway set up on a side street features a Ferris wheel, merry-go-round, and half a dozen other rides designed to amuse and confuse.

Evenings there are at least four outdoor music stages, usually at cafés: typically these might include one devoted to blues, one folk, and one Mexican. Keep an eye out for some big names, too. The Stephen Barry Blues Band shows up almost every year; Mr. Barry got his start in St Jovite and likes to help make the Jovi-Foire a success. Several stands serve beer as well as soft drinks, since alcohol is permitted in the streets during the festival. As I sipped a beer near the folk stage, an 80-year-old woman sang one of the naughtiest songs I've ever heard! Needless to say, the crowd went wild.

In 1996, the Sky Hawks parachutists made an appearance. Twice daily on Friday and Saturday, the 14 jumpers of the Canadian Forces Parachute Team fell from the sky, spinning and turning, performing acrobatic parachute stunts. In between jumps, the team mingled with the crowd, answering questions. You could even help them fold their parachutes! This event was a real crowd-pleaser and will almost certainly be repeated.

The big fundraiser is the duck race that closes the festivities on the final Sunday night. At 4:30 p.m. sharp, 2,500 ducks are released onto the Rivière du Diable (Devil's River) at the north end of town. One kilometre later, they are routed into a series of ever-narrowing channels, until finally just one duck squeezes through. Whoever has the ticket corresponding to the winning duck receives a whopping $5,000 prize. (A total of $10,000 in cash prizes is given away.) Sadly, the ducks are of the plastic kiddy-pool variety, not the feathered flying-away kind.

We never did find a "Neolithic-looking cliff with a cave facing westwards overlooking a valley with no buildings but a river" suitable for a 10-second scene in a pickle commercial. But the Jovi-Foire was an equally rewarding discovery!

SEASON AND HOURS
Thurs–Sun, in mid-July (July 17–20 in 1997).

FEES
Free. Small fees for some activities.

INFORMATION
St Jovite Chamber of Commerce (819) 425-8441.

DIRECTIONS
Take Highway 15 (Laurentian Autoroute) north to where it ends at St Agathe. Continue on Route 117 another 31 km to St Jovite.

Hiking and Picnicking in
Parc Mt Tremblant
(Pimbina Section)
St Donat
DRIVING TIME: 2 HR

Photo: Pierre Parliot / Parc Mont Tremblant

To most people, Mont Tremblant means skiing and snowboarding. But Mont Tremblant Provincial Park, of which the ski centre is a part, covers a very large area and offers a variety of landscapes and activities. If sweet-smelling woods, crisp mountain air, and unspoiled wilderness are to your liking, take a trip into the easterly section, called Pimbina. Here, sharp peaks mellow into soft ridges, and rounded valleys cradle deep blue lakes. You can hike along numerous trails, picnic by a waterfall, or simply drive along a lovely country road.

A tourist bureau in St Donat can provide information on hikes both inside and outside the park. (Apparently there are a number of trails outside the park well worth investigating—including one with a view of Montreal!) Inside the park, the visitor's centre will get you started on a pleasant day's

LAURENTIANS

outing, winter, spring, summer, or fall.

I spent a very enjoyable couple of hours one autumn weekend strolling along the well-maintained 2.5-km Sentier L'Envol (Lift-Off Trail). It wanders through yellow birch, sumac, and maple forest, past enormous moss-covered rocks deposited randomly by glaciers 20,000 years ago, when the whole area was under 3,000 m of ice. The last stretch is a 100-m staircase up along a damp, mossy cliffside. There are two lookouts on the summit overlooking the narrow, densley forested Pimbina Valley, with a view of three distant lakes.

This is a very special hike for two other reasons. First, a booklet available from a box at the start of the trail describes the flora and geology at each stage of your journey. Second, this is the only trail with (dry) toilets at the bottom and top, and picnic tables at the summit.

There are another couple of self-guided trails: Lac des Femmes (Women's Lake) and Lac Atocas (Cranberry Lake), both in the Diable (Devil) section.

Another 2 or 3 km farther north along the narrow roller-coaster country road is a place seemingly infested with rats. There is the tiny Lac de Rats (Rat Lake), the Ruisseaux des Rats (Rat Stream), and finally the Chute des Rats (Rat Falls). But don't worry, the rats in question are of the charming muskrat (*rat muské*) variety, not the nasty back-alley cheese-eaters. Maybe they just ran out of space on the signs.

The Chute des Rats falls are a couple of hundred metres from the parking lot, where there are flush toilets and running (but non-potable) water. A sandy beach at the foot of the falls makes a nice spot for a picinic. Children will enjoy scrambling across the large square granite boulders that front the falls like a giant tumble-down staircase. To the right of the falls is a real staircase leading to the top. Those short of time or wind can take heart: the view from the bottom is better.

The base of the falls and washrooms are wheelchair accessible.

SEASON AND HOURS
All year.

FEES
Free.

INFORMATION
(819) 424-2954.

DIRECTIONS
Take Highway 15 (Laurentian Autoroute) north to exit 89. From there, follow Route 329 north through St Donat. The entrance to Pimbina is 7 km north of St Donat. If you have time, take the spectacularly scenic Route 125. This is a gorgeous divided highway, with little traffic.

Lanaudière

Lanaudière remains largely undiscovered by Montrealers. This is a shame, since it is a region of great natural beauty. On  its western edge it is a high, rolling country of equal parts dense forest and tamed pasture. To the east, the farmland of the St Lawrence Valley comes head to head with the exposed granite of the Canadian Shield.

 Throughout the region, frothing rapids and tumbling waterfalls cut through some charming parks. Best of all, even its farthest reaches are only just an hour or two from Montreal.

In and around Rawdon, there are waterfalls, rapids, and swimming holes. Earle Moore's Canadiana Village is another hidden treasure not far from this pleasant town. North of Joliette, you return to mountains as rugged as the Laurentians. This rocky and heavily wooded hinterland features winding roads, exposed cliffs, rushing rivers, and picturesque valleys reminiscent of the Rockies. There, the Montagne Coupée  (Cut Mountain) provides excellent four-season outdoor activities, including horseback riding. The village of St Jean de Matha conceals an interesting museum, and a terrific park with waterfalls. Farther

 north, the Parc Régional des Sept Chutes offers splendid views and rugged hiking.

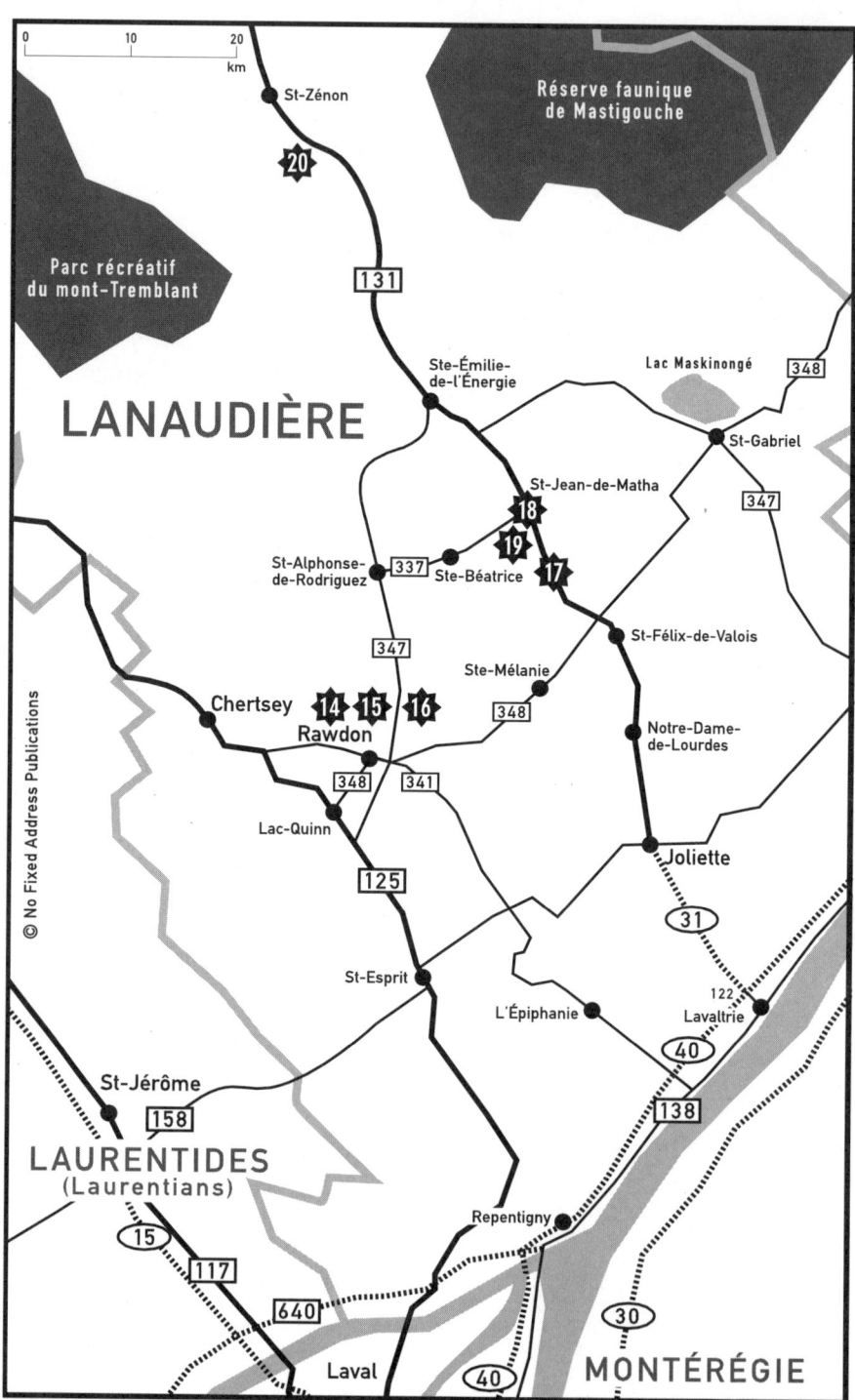

LANAUDIÈRE

Trip Destinations

14 Parc des Chutes Dorwin
(Dorwin Falls)
Rawdon
(514) 834-2251
p.46

15 Rawdon Rapids and Rawdon
Municipal Beach
Rawdon
Rapids: (514) 834-2251
Beach: (514) 834-4149
p.48

16 Earle Moore's Canadiana Village
Rawdon
(514) 834-4135
p.50

17 La Montagne Coupée
St Jean de Matha
(514) 886-3845
p.52

18 Louis Cyr Museum
St Jean de Matha
(514) 886-2777
p.54

19 Parc Régional des Chutes Monte à
Peine et des Dalles (Waterfalls)
St Jean de Matha/St Béatrix/
St Mélanie
(514) 883-2245
p.56

20 Parc Régional des Sept Chutes
(Waterfalls)
St Zénon
(514) 884-5437
p.58

Tourist Information

Lanaudière Tourist Association
(514) 834-2535, (800) 363-2788

Rawdon Chamber of Commerce
(514) 834-2282

St Emélie de l'Energie Town Hall
(514) 886-3823

Get Outta Town! **45**

Parc des
Chutes Dorwin
(Dorwin Falls)
Rawdon
DRIVING TIME: 1 HR 15 MIN

R awdon is a mid-sized country town on the western edge of the high, rolling region called Lanaudière. It may well be the most ethnically diverse town in Canada, with 35 ethnic groups living together in harmony, and each one swearing the land reminds them of the old country. Rawdon is surrounded by great natural beauty. Two rivers, the Ouareau and the Rouge, wind through it, and the area is renowned for its tall pine trees. It is also well known for the remarkable Dorwin Falls, which are almost in the town itself.

Early one spring I went north to Rawdon in search of a place to watch the spring thaw whisk away the last traces of winter. It would be hard to find

46 Get Outta Town!

a place better than Dorwin Falls. Any time of year, you are bound to see an incredible torrent of water, cutting through a deep, narrow gorge, topped on either side by tall pine trees.

There are two main lookouts at the falls. At the head, a sturdy wooden platform extends beyond the steep cliff and over the gorge. Here the falls are close to eye level, and you can look down to the frothing waters about 30 m below. Stairs and a path lead down to another lookout a little deeper in the gorge. Both lookouts have chain-link fences, making them safe for small children and camera bags, and both provide the excitement of roaring water, gentle mists, and the scent of the forest.

A sign posted on the lower lookout tells the legend surrounding the falls: Once upon a time there was a beautiful Indian princess, Hiawatha. Much loved by all, she was pursued romantically by the evil Nippisingue. When she rejected his advances, he pushed her into a stream. She drowned, and the stream was so angry at being used in this way, it turned magically into the present day torrent of white water. When the sorcerer Manitou found out, he was furious, too, and turned Nippisingue to stone. To this day the evil Nippisingue's profile can seen jutting out over the falls.

Whether you believe the legend or not is up to you, but from the lower lookout the profile of a human face can easily be seen against the falls. This may be the only face-in-the-rocks in the world that can be discerned without the need for self-hypnosis.

The tall pine stand at the entrance to the park is a great place for a picnic, and dozens of tables are set out in the cool, sweet-smelling shade. It is conveniently close to the parking lot, modern washrooms, and a snack bar. There is also a large grassy area for playing. And it's all far enough away from the falls that you don't have to worry about mishaps.

Both lookouts are wheelchair accessible, though the path to the lower lookout is rather steep.

SEASON AND HOURS
9 a.m.–7 p.m., every day, mid-May–mid-Oct.

FEES
Adults $2, children 5–12 $1, under 5 free, parking $2.

INFORMATION
Rawdon Chamber of Commerce (514) 834-2282.

DIRECTIONS
Take Highway 15 (Laurentian Autoroute) north to Highway 640. Head west on the 640 to Route 125. Follow the 125 north to Quinn Lake. From there, take Route 337 towards Rawdon. Dorwin Falls are on Route 337 just before Rawdon.

Swimming at the
Rawdon Rapids
or Rawdon Municipal Beach
Rawdon
DRIVING TIME: 1 HR 15 MIN

Photo: Luc Landry / Lanaudière Tourist Association

A few kilometres north of Rawdon, a lovely wooded park hugs the edge of the Ouareau River. Officially named the Halte Cascades—the stopping place by the rapids—it is known locally as the **Rawdon Rapids**. In spring, the rocks that form the rapids are completely covered by a raging torrent of water. But the park sees more human activity in the summer, when it becomes a veritable pilgrimage site for sun-worshippers, bathers, and young lovers.

In the warm season, half a dozen fingers of wide, flat granite are exposed, stretching unevenly across the river from shore to shore, water swirling gently around them. On a sunny weekend day, they are crawling with people. This is an extremely youthful scene—the average age appears to be about eighteen—but although there is always music, it's generally at a reasonable level. And

48 Get Outta Town!

LANAUDIÈRE

though signs forbid swimming and alcohol, there is no shortage of either.

There is a gravel parking lot at the entrance, near the restrooms. (There are no changing rooms, so you might want to come ready for bathing.) Or you can park along the winding road leading to a plateau above the river. Shaded by the 18-m pine trees common in the Rawdon area, this is an ideal spot for a picnic.

A long wooden staircase leads down to the river's edge, and a small footbridge takes you across a narrow rush of water. There are no lifeguards, since swimming is officially forbidden, but it is a lovely spot for a dip, and thankfully, officials turn a blind eye. At the base of the rapids, the river widens into a deep pool with barely any current. The more maniacal enjoy jumping in at a spot by the bridge where the water courses madly down a channel.

Be careful crossing the rocks, as they can be deceptively slippery. A good pair of sneakers will help. Staff are quick to clean up, but keep an eye out for broken glass. (Unlike most beaches, this one has no rule against bottles.)

If you prefer your swimming holes a little more civilized, visit the **Rawdon Municipal Beach**. Just off the town centre, this clean, sandy beach leads steeply down to Lake Rawdon on the Rouge River. Supervised swimming, a large parking lot, and modern sanitation facilities make this a very pleasant beach catering more to families.

Rawdon Rapids
SEASON AND HOURS
Mid-May–mid-Oct.
FEES
$6 per car; $3 per motorcycle.
INFORMATION
(514) 834-4149 in season.
Rawdon Chamber of Commerce
(514) 834-2282.
DIRECTIONS
Take Highway 15 (Laurentian Autoroute) north to the Highway 640. Head east on the 640 to Route 125. Follow the 125 north past Rawdon to where it crosses Route 341. Turn right onto Route 341 (towards Rawdon). The rapids are a short distance along the road, on the right-hand side.

Rawdon Municipal Beach
SEASON AND HOURS
June 24–mid-Oct.
FEES
$6 per car.
INFORMATION
Rawdon Chamber of Commerce
(514) 834-2282.
DIRECTIONS
Take Highway 15 (Laurentian Autoroute) north to Highway 640. Head east on the 640 to Route 125. Follow the 125 north to Quinn Lake. From there, take Route 337 into Rawdon. Turn left on Rue St Marie, then right on 6th Ave.

Earle Moore's
Canadiana Village
Rawdon
DRIVING TIME: 1 HR 20 MIN

Sometime in the '50s, the late Mr. and Mrs. Moore, avid antique shoppers, were out driving in rural Quebec when they noticed two moving vans parked outside an antique store. The owner of the store explained that whenever she purchased a spinning wheel or crib she loaded it into one of the vans. Once she had 100 spinning wheels or cribs, she called a dealer in the States who took them south, to be sold as Americana.

Out of the Moore's desire to protect our heritage, and starting with an old schoolhouse from Rawdon (acquired as a guesthouse), Earle Moore's Canadiana Village has grown to include 55 buildings and displays; it is now considered the largest private collection of Canadiana in the country. But such a description overemphasizes its historic role. It also provides a delightful opportunity to spend an afternoon strolling beautifully tended grounds, high on a hillside, with sweeping views of the ridges and hills of Lanaudière.

The buildings are arranged like a little pioneer village, with a main street, a green, and a couple of country lanes. There is not lot of hustle and bustle on this trip through time. You can stroll from house to house at your own pace. Friendly, perfectly bilingual guides in period costume are on hand to answer questions or explain just what it is they're doing with that little thingamajig.

LANAUDIÈRE

If the church, schoolhouse, and other buildings seem familiar, it is because over 55 films have been made in the village, including scenes from *In the Name of the Father and the Son*.

Grandma's House is a special attraction. This tiny 200-year-old country house is decorated, year-round, for Christmas, with old-fashioned toys under a tree. On occasion, a real-life grandma is in the kitchen explaining all the strange ustensils.

There is also a Doll House with 120 dolls and a Music House with various instruments, where a professional musician plays on weekends. Kids will get a kick out of the Town Jail, complete with prisoner—is he sleeping, or is it just a mannequin? On a hot day, take a stroll down shady Lover's Lane. You can even tour the home of Mr. and Mr. Moore-McDonald, the daughter and son-in-law of the founders, to view some priceless antiques, including a desk that belonged to Prime Minister Sir Wilfred Laurier.

In the summer months, a number of houses feature demonstrations of traditional crafts, including spinning, candle dipping, and wool dyeing. You can also get a real two-bit shave with a straight razor (if you dare) at the barber shop.

Picknickers are welcome in the village. For snacks, you can enjoy old-fashioned ice cream at the ice-cream parlour or knock back lemonade in a real saloon, complete with swinging doors and brass spittoons. For a great country meal, cup of coffee, or homemade pastries, stop in at the streamside restaurant. The converted grist mill is a cosy place, complete with a giant water wheel turning outside its windows.

By the way, Mr. and Mrs. Moore-MacDonald have a new rule now. They still collect Canadiana, but they have vowed not to bring home any more buildings!

The village is wheelchair accessible with assistance.

SEASON AND HOURS
10:30 a.m.–5 p.m., Tues–Sun (except when closed for filming). Since a comfortable tour takes 2–3 hr, visitors are only reluctantly admitted after 3 p.m.

FEES
Adults $9.25; youth $6.50; under 5 free.

INFORMATION
(514) 834-4135.

DIRECTIONS
Take Highway 15 (Laurentian Autoroute) north to Highway 640. Head east on the 640 to Route 125. Follow the 125 north to Quinn Lake. From there, take Route 337 into Rawdon. Turn left on Rue St Marie, then right on 6th Ave, and left on Anderson/Chemin du lac Morgan. The village is several kilometres outside of Rawdon, on the right-hand side.

Note: Ownership in transition. Please call before visiting.

La Montagne Coupée
near St Jean de Matha

DRIVING TIME: 1 HR 10 MIN

Photo: La Montagne Coupée

Now here's a well-named mountain. From certain vantage points, Montagne Coupée does indeed appear as if half of it has been cut away and carted off. But the beauty of the mountain itself and the splendid views from its demi-summit are the least of the reasons to visit. Especially popular when the surrounding hills and forested ridges come to life with autumn colours, this privately run recreation centre has something for everyone, all year round.

Activities include horseback riding, mountain biking, roller-blading, and hiking in summer, and cross-country skiing, snowshoeing, kicksledding, and dogsledding in winter. If you're too pooped to drive home, you can even spend the night in the luxury of the inn atop the mountain.

The base of the uncut side of the mountain is the focus for all day-trip activities. A modern and functional single-storey visitor's centre is where you arrange for trail passes and equipment rental. The staff is friendly and helpful, and the rental equipment is top-notch. The visitor's centre has washrooms and a cafeteria, and sit-down meals are available at the Restaurant Patrimoine, serving healthy fare, crêpes, and fondues.

There are hiking trails for all levels of experience and stamina, with numerous observation towers overlooking the surrounding countryside. Trail 9 is a popular choice, leading through the woods and alongside the

LANAUDIÈRE

winding Assomption River, as are the summit trails, with marvellous views off the edge of the 100-m cliff.

For mountain bikers there are two types of trails: maintained trails for casual bikers, and rugged ones for those with elbows of steel. You can rent mountain bikes by the hour, half day, and full day.

Montagne Coupée has a well-organized equestrian centre, with 40 western-saddle horses. Join a group for an hour-long guided ride through the woods and up the mountain trails, or go alone on longer rides. Lessons are available. Reservations are required for self-guided tours and recommended for hour-long outings, especially in high season (autumn).

Something really special is the new 2-km paved roller-blading track. The figure eight winds over hill and dale, and through the woods at the base of the mountain. It looks like a lot of fun, if somewhat challenging.

The view from behind the inn is worth mentioning twice. It looks westward over mixed forest typical of the undeveloped Lanaudière countryside. On a clear day you can see Montreal, and the view is marred only by hydro-electric towers far below. You can stroll a 2-km trail around the summit (or ski it in winter). The summit trail is delicately lit in the evening.

In winter, 85 km of ski trails dominate the scene: 65 km are groomed for shared use by classic and skate-skiers, while 20 km are left untouched for backwoods adventures. One-hour dogsledding trips are increasingly popular, and overnight guests can skate on the little pond near the inn. Non-skiers can rent a kicksled (*luge finlandaise*) for some on-trail fun or snowshoes for off-trail escapades.

SEASON AND HOURS
All year.

FEES
Summer
Hiking trail fee $1.
Horseback riding: Adults $13.75, children $10.50 1 hr; $25 2 hr; $37 half day, $62.50 full day.
Mountain biking: Trail fee $4.56; rental $10 per hr, $25 half day, $35 full day.
Winter
Ski trail fee: General $8.50, golden-agers $6.50, children $3.25.
Snowshoe trail fee $6.50; snowshoe rental $6.
Dogsledding $50 1 hr. Rates slightly lower on weekdays.

INFORMATION
(514) 886-3845.

DIRECTIONS
Take Highway 40 (Trans-Canada) east to exit 122 (Joliette). Head north on Route 31/131 to Joliette, and follow signs to La Montagne Coupée, halfway between St Félix de Valois and St Jean de Matha, on the left-hand side.

Musée Louis-Cyr
(Strongman Louis Cyr Museum)
St Jean de Matha
DRIVING TIME: 1 HR 15 MIN

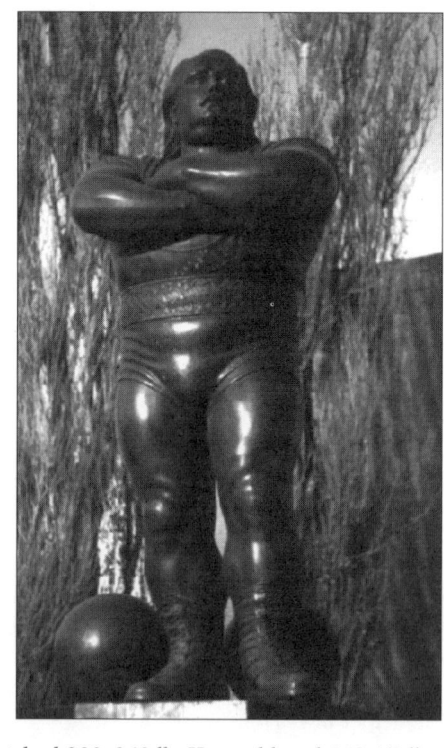

If you drive east along St Jacques Street in Montreal and follow it under the Ville Marie Expressway into St Henri, you may notice an unobtrusive statue in a small park at the fork of St Jacques and St Antoine streets. It portrays a shortish but very broad, muscular man standing with his arms folded across his bare chest. This is Quebec strongman (and St Henri policeman) Louis Cyr, perhaps the strongest man the world has ever seen.

An Acadian born in Napierville in 1863, Cyr was big from the start. Reputedly 18 lb at birth, he grew to 5' 8" and at the height of his career weighed 300–360 lb. He could curl 162 1/2 lb in one hand 36 times in a row, and lift 553 lb with a single finger (without bending his knees). One of his crowd-pleasers was to load 18 men onto a giant plate, for a total of over 3,000 lb, and carry it on his back. The list of his accomplishments goes on and on. Suffice to say that he offered

54 Get Outta Town!

$25,000 to anyone who could beat him in a test of strength, and no one ever saw a penny.

He had a successful circus boasting Siamese twins, acrobats, a fat man, and a tall man, among others—plus himself as star attraction. Though from a family of 17 children, he had only a son and daughter. He got his strength from his mother, and passed it on to his daughter. At the age of 12, she joined Cyr's circus, performing an act that involved lifting and holding her mother aloft in one hand.

Cyr didn't drink to excess or smoke, but he did eat plenty of meat—up to 10 lb of red meat at each meal—and drank a gallon or two of milk every day. Unfortunately, his hearty appetite and peculiar diet undoubtedly led to his early demise. Cyr died in Montreal in 1912, at the young age of 42, of Bright's disease, a degenerative disease of the liver. He was a strict vegetarian in the end.

The Louis Cyr Museum opened in the summer of 1996, in St Jean de Matha, the town the strongman called home. It is a cosy room in the back end of the town hall. The museum, run by the local chamber of commerce, tells the story of his life with large panels, photos, and artifacts from his rich career. The collection includes a number of weights as well, though most are in the private collection of modern day health advocate (and Montrealer) Ben Weider. The collection is impressive, nevertheless, featuring travelling cases, various weights, and his strongman belt bearing the word "Fortissimo" and decorated with maple leaves. The collection will surely grow as word of the museum's existence spreads.

For a great snack in a lovely setting, visit the Amont La Côte, an outdoor café right next to the museum with its tables in a charming little garden. The menu includes various local sausages, including the Louis Cyr. It isn't strong, but you can always have it with strong mustard!

SEASON AND HOURS
10 a.m.–6 p.m., every day, June 24–Thanksgiving weekend.

FEES
Free.

INFORMATION
(514) 886-2779.

DIRECTIONS
Take Highway 40 (Trans-Canada) east to exit 122 (Joliette). Head north on Route 31/131 to Joliette, then continue north on the 131 to St Jean de Matha. Leave the highway at the Esso station, turning onto Rue Principale. The museum is at 184 Rue St Louise. For a much prettier drive that is not much longer, take Route 125 north to Rawdon, then Route 348 east to the 131.

Waterfalls at Parc Régional des Chutes Monte à Peine et des Dalles
St Jean de Matha/ St Béatrix/St Mélanie

DRIVING TIME: 1 HR 20 MIN

According to the signs and brochures in the village, about 3 km southwest of St Jean de Matha, there should be an entrance to a small park that contains not one, but three lovely waterfalls linked by an 8-km trail. Though it is clearly signposted from the village, as you follow Route 337 west out of town, you have to wonder just where these falls could be. For the most part, the landscape consists of neatly tended fields—some crops, but mainly dairy pasture—and rolls gently, but not enough to suggest waterfalls. There are ridges in the distance, but they are certainly farther off than the promised 3 km.

Just when you're beginning to think you've been duped, another sign points to the left. And when you turn southwest onto the gravel Rang St Louise west, the road suddenly drops away beneath you. Then, instead of levelling out like a good road, it continues to plunge steeply downwards, twisting and turning back upon itself like an insane snake (or a road through the Alps). Aha! The falls must be this-a-way.

A short ride later, the road does level out, and a humble wooden booth marks the entrance to an unspoiled and charming park. Whether it is the journey there, or simply the sound of distant water heard from the parking lot, there is a wonderful sense of foreshadowing in approaching the Assomption River and the Monte à Peine Falls.

Like many smaller parks in Quebec, Chutes Monte à Peine et des Dalles Regional Park is run by local municipalities—in this case, St Jean de Matha, St Béatrix, and St Mélanie. Each has its own entrance. St Jean de Matha and St Mélanie provide access to the Monte à Peine and Desjardins falls, while St Beatrix leads to the Dalles Falls. Trails connect the areas.

The trails in the St Jean de Matha part of the park are wide and easy to walk, with sturdy wooden staircases leading alongside the falls and down the river. There are excellent views from three superb wooden lookouts and the wide bridge that leads across the river at the head of the falls. Those with small children needn't worry. The falls are fierce, but the lookouts are childproof, as is the bridge.

Monte à Peine roughly translates as "hard to get over" and from the bridge at their head the falls don't appear to deserve their name. But as you descend the wooden steps below, the inspiration becomes apparent. The falls are impressive. Though low in profile, they are about 45 m at their widest, flowing over a granite wedding-cake formation that juts irregularly out of the river. About two thirds of the water roars madly down to one side, while the rest tumbles somewhat more calmly to the other.

A trail connects the three falls, but ask a fellow visitor which one it is, since at least one trail leads to a dead end, and there don't seem to be any maps available. Picnickers are welcome, but there are no toilets.

SEASON AND HOURS
Mid-May–mid-Oct.

FEES
$3 per person.

INFORMATION
(514) 883-2245.

DIRECTIONS
Take Highway 40 (Trans-Canada) east to exit 122 (Joliette). Head north on Route 31/131 to Joliette, then continue north on the 131 to St Jean de Matha. Leave the highway at the Esso station, turning onto Rue Principale. Turn left on Rue St Louise, and follow Route 337 west in the direction of St Béatrix. A short distance later, turn left onto Rang St Louise west. The Monte à Peine Falls are 3 km from the village centre.
Continue along Route 337 west to Rang des Dalles for the entrance to the Dalles Falls area. The St Mélanie area is along Route 348, 6 km south of St Jean de Matha off Route 131.

Hiking in Parc Régional des Sept Chutes
St Zénon

DRIVING TIME: 1 HR 40 MIN

Photo: Luc Landry / Lanaudière Tourist Association

Contrary to what the name indicates, there are not seven waterfalls in Sept Chutes Regional Park. There is just one, and it flows mainly in the spring. But what the park has in abundance are rugged trails around picturesque lakes, up a densely wooded mountain, and along high cliffs. If you like vigorous hikes, challenging trails, crisp mountain air, and the reward of spectacular views, Sept Chutes Park is just the place.

Even if you don't, the trip there is well worthwhile. The road from Joliette to St Jean de Matha is not uninteresting, but north of St Jean de Matha you leave the farmland quite suddenly behind for a countryside of astonishing natural beauty. The road rises steeply as you enter an area known as the Matawinie, then narrows as it is squeezed between the shoulders of the mountains. Each bend in the road reveals a new delight. Around one corner, it opens up onto a wide, flat, treeless valley. Around another is a cottage clinging tightly to the mountain over the river. Rapids, small waterfalls, wetlands, and ponds mark the distance as you travel north, guided by the Noire River.

LANAUDIÈRE

You can't miss the entrance to the Sept Chutes; it is one of the few places where the road widens enough to park, and there are two roadside parking lots.

You'll need sturdy hiking boots, and perhaps a walking stick to hike comfortably here. The trails are poorly maintained and the few staircases may be scary, but don't be discouraged.

On the way to Lake Guy, you will come across the Chute du Voile de la Mariée (Bridal Veil Falls). In autumn, it is a flow that might, in dim light at a full gallop, be considered a waterfall. But during the spring run-off, the steep streambed sustains a strong flow of white water resembling a bride's veil. Whatever the season, it is a great place to take a breather and replenish your drinking bottle from the continuously flowing fountain fed by the stream.

When I visited the park in late September, the leaves were already past their prime, but the landscape had all the ingredients for a great autumn hike: mixed maple, beech, and fir, with hills for display and lakes for contrast. The hiking was super. The ridge trail that leads around the crown of Mount Brossard has a spectacular view westward off a sheer unguarded cliff, rising 150 m above Lake Rémi. If you are short on time, you can reach the cliffs in about 1 hr by taking the most direct route. If you are in less of a rush, you can take 2 or 3 hr by heading out counterclockwise from the hut at the entrance. The climb in that direction is hilly but not as steep, and you end your day with the best view.

In autumn, take care not to start out on the trails too late, since they can be difficult in the fading light. There are no facilities other than dry toilets. Various trails take from 50 min to 3 hr to hike.

By the way, the seven waterfalls are indeed on the Noire River, but a little farther south, just north of St Emélie de l'Énergie. The Matawinie Trail leads 3.8 km from Route 131 to Lake Kaël, past the Tombereau (Tipcart) and Cheval Blanc (White Horse) falls, a couple of the more noteworthy ones. There is a 19-km trail to Sept Chutes Park.

SEASON AND HOURS
8 a.m.–5 p.m., every day, May–Oct.

FEES
$2 per person.

INFORMATION
Sept Chutes Park (514) 884-5437;
St Emélie de l'Énergie town hall
(514) 886-3823.

DIRECTIONS
Take Highway 40 (Trans-Canada) east to exit 122 (Joliette). Head north on Route 31/131 to Joliette, then continue north on the 131. The park is approximately 32 km past St Jean de Matha, on the left-hand side of the road.

Eastern Townships

The Eastern Townships have been neatly described as combining English charm with French joie de vivre. This delightful region is noted for the serene beauty of its lakes, the tidiness of its farms, and the lure of its country roads.

Nestled in the rolling hills and farmland of the Townships you'll find postcard-perfect towns that look strikingly like New England villages, with Protestant churches, white clapboard homes, and riverside pubs. This should come as no surprise, since the Townships were settled largely by Americans loyal to the Crown, who fled the

Photo: Eastern Townships Tourist Association

United States at the time of the Revolution. But the passage of time has melded traditions, and a lively culture unique to the region flourishes, as you will see.

Hiking with llamas or touring artists' studios; being lulled by Gregorian chanting or exploring irresistible country museums; touring a vineyard or enjoying a county fair: whether you prefer a quiet day alone in the country or a busy day in a bustling tourist community, there's always a lot to do.

Photo: Eastern Townships Tourist Association

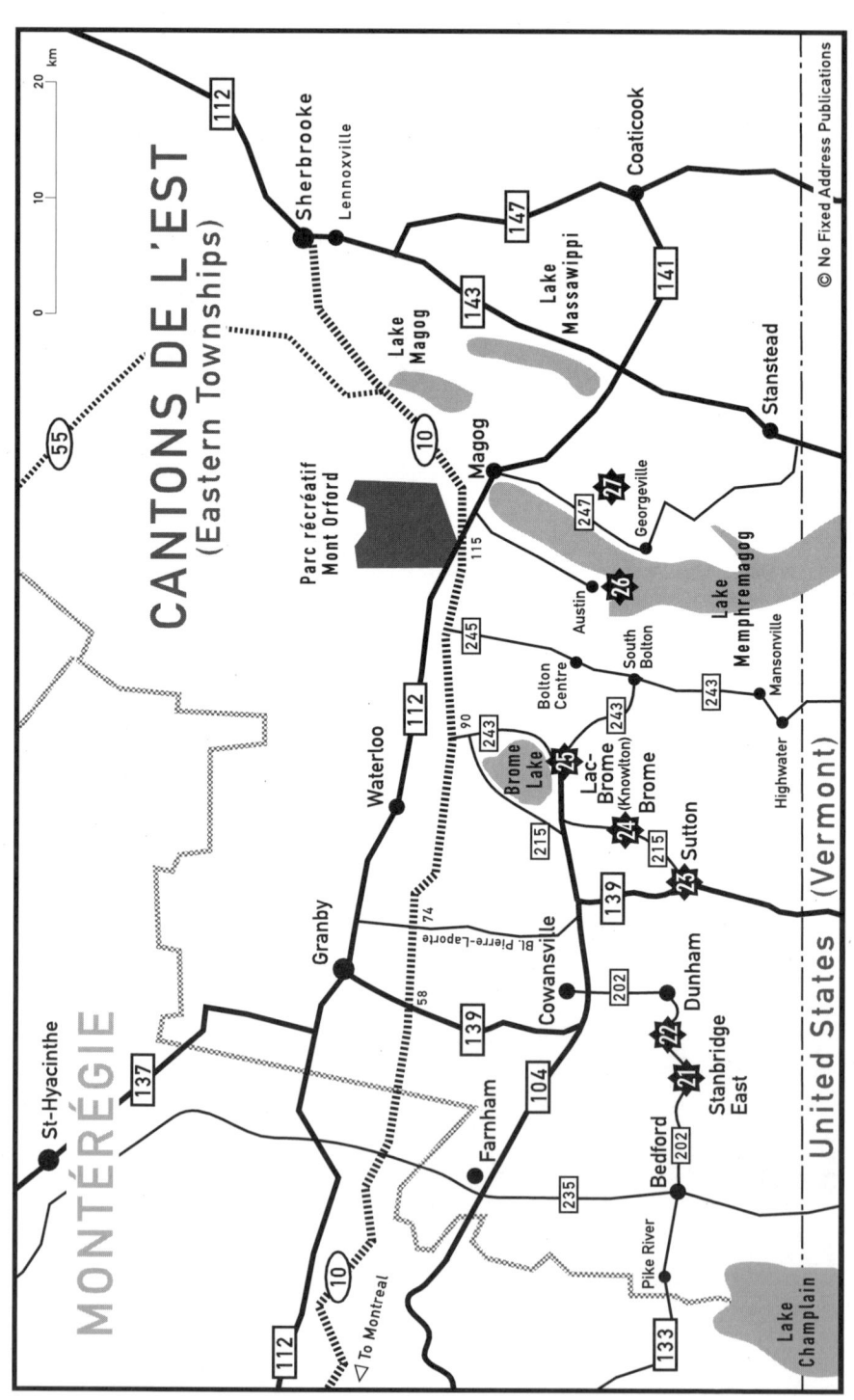

EASTERN TOWNSHIPS

Trip Destinations

21 Missisquoi Historical Society
Museum
Stanbridge East
(514) 248-3153
p.64

22 Wine Tour of the Eastern Townships
Bedford–Dunham
p.66

23 Living Museum of Llamas
(Llamadu)
Mount Sutton
(514) 538-5521
p.68

24 Brome County Fair
Near Brome
(514) 242-EXPO (3976)
p.70

25 Brome County Historical Society
Museum
Knowlton
(514) 243-6782
p.72

26 St Benoît du Lac Abbey
Near Magog
(819) 843-4080
p.74

27 Circuit des Arts Memphrémagog
(Memphremagog Art Tour)
Lake Memphremagog
(800) 267-2744, (819) 843-2744
p.76

Tourist Information

Eastern Townships Tourist Association
(800) 355-5755, (819) 820-2020

Knowlton Tourist Bureau
(514) 242-2870

Magog–Orford Tourist Bureau
(800) 267-2744, (819) 843-2744

Missisquoi
Historical Society Museum
Stanbridge East

DRIVING TIME: 1 HR 15 MIN

Crossing the bridge over the calm Pike River and entering Stanbridge East on a hot summer's day, you get a sense that this must be what 19th-century life in the Eastern Townships was like at its best. An old mill stands on the river's edge, its water wheel slowly turning. Picnickers lounge in the shady park separated from the river by a long fieldstone wall. A few people are gathered for cold beer on the wide verandah of the waterside pub.

Besides simply strolling the riverside streets and lanes of Stanbridge East, the best way to time-travel in this pretty town is by way of the friendly, comfortable Missisquoi Museum. There's plenty to fascinate young and old alike.

The heart of the museum is the Cornell Mill. Built in 1830, this three-storey brick mill, complete with a working water wheel, houses the main collection. The ground floor replicates the interior of a late 19th-century country home. Each year the "rooms" are redone to examine a new facet of Victorian life. Keep an eye out for homey touches like the mouse by the potbelly stove, and for intriguing wreaths and miniature floral arrangements made entirely of human hair!

Children will love the upper floor, where antique toys are on display, including a hand-carved circus set and a giant doll's house straight out of Mary Poppins. They will also get a kick out of the river-level basement, with its re-creations of a cobbler's workshop, a dentist's office, a one-room schoolhouse, and other aspects of village life. Don't forget to take a peek down through the trapdoor at the old millstone and the water just beneath.

Hodge's Store, a 5 min walk up the street, is the second of the museum's buildings. Built in 1840, this old-time general store is bursting with goods spanning the century it served the community. A host of items will fascinate you with their primitive ingenuity—or make you feel old. Wire corn poppers, stove-top toasters, and Carter's Little Liver Pills stand next to the shapeless woollen bathing suits of yesteryear.

A little farther along is Bill's Barn. Originally a dairy, the building now houses a large collection of farming machinery. Be alert for some unusual items. Tucked away among the ploughs and carriages are a hearse on runners and several dog-powered treadmills, including one resembling a giant gerbil wheel.

Farmer's Park, across the river from the Cornell Mill, is an ideal spot for a picnic. The park is shaded and landscaped, and offers a beautiful view of the river, the falls, and the mill. There is a low dry-stone wall where the park meets the river. The Farmer's Wall, as it is called, is built entirely without mortar, and commemorates the annual chore of clearing stones from the fields. A brass sundial on a pedestal pays homage to the 30 or so Loyalist families who settled in the region prior to 1830.

Nearby Owl Hoot Maple Farm on Ross Road sells soft and chewy maple cream and other maple products that make nice picnic treats. Another site of interest is the aquatic plant nursery, À Fleur d'Eau, just outside of town, where half a dozen different styles of garden ponds are on display.

SEASON AND HOURS
10 a.m.–5 p.m., every day, last Sun in May to second Sun in Oct.

FEES
Adults $3, seniors and groups $2.50, students and children $1.

INFORMATION
Museum (514) 248-3153.

DIRECTIONS
Take Highway 10 (Eastern Townships Autoroute) east to exit 22. Follow Highway 35 south to Iberville, where it joins Route 133. Continue south on Route 133 to Pike River, then head east on Route 202 through Bedford. Seven kilometres east of Bedford, follow the clearly marked signs to Stanbridge East.

Wine Tour of the
Eastern Townships
Bedford to Dunham
DRIVING TIME: 1 HR 20 MIN

A wine tour of Quebec? If that sounds about as likely as an artichoke tour of the Arctic, you're in for a surprise. About two dozen wineries account for over 200,000 bottles a year, from grapes raised, pressed, and bottled in Quebec. One 10-km rolling stretch of country road boasts a cluster of five wineries. Touring the vineyards and sampling the wares is a pleasant pastime, made even more pleasant by the warmth and friendliness of the owners, who are eager to share their love of wine.

On the outskirts of Dunham, a farmhouse dating from 1836 is home to **Les Arpents de Neige**, where not even the dog, Seyval, has escaped the influence of the grape. Les Arpents sells three wines, including the area's only rosé.

A tour ($3.50) takes about an hour and includes tastings. The dining room's menu lists lamb and smoked duck. A gift shop features handicrafts, such as beeswax candles, dried flowers, and bath salts. Garden-fresh gladiolas are sold, plus a small but very aromatic local melon.

The hilltop **Vignoble Les Trois Clochers** is named for its view of three church bell towers. The newest vineyard in the area offers no tour, but photos on the walls of the reception area and boutique—built on top of the winery—depict the art of wine making, from planting to bottling. For 50 cents, you can sample one of the best Seyvals on the strip or the area's only strawberry wine. The boutique sells homemade jams and jellies, as well as colourful dried flowers.

A stone archway marks the entrance to **Les Côtes d'Ardoise**, whose heavy wooden doors are reminiscent of European monastic wineries. Vines frame the barn-slat building on the steep slate hill from which the vineyard gets its name. Les Côtes produces the largest selection in the Dunham area, including a much coveted ice-wine. (Ice-wine is made from a grape that is allowed to freeze and thaw repeatedly, while still on the vine.) A large, shaded picnic area is ideal for do-it-yourselfers, and the vineyard can cater to groups with advance notice. A tour costs $4.50.

In 1990, Pierre Genesse and Marie-Claude Lizotte bought a stable set in an apple orchard and created **Les Blancs Coteaux** (the white slopes), complete with a spicily scented country store.

They sell two white wines and two European-style ciders. You can put together your own picnic basket of Townships produce or buy one ready-made. The picnic for two ($19.95) includes a Seyval mustard, a hot French loaf or two, cheddar cheese, and pork and duck pâté. Topping it off is a decadent goat's-milk chocolate fudge from East Farnham. Don't forget the wine!

The final vineyard on the tour is the **Vignoble de l'Orpailleur** (the gold-washer), the largest and most successful of the cottage vineyards in Quebec. L'Orpailleur produces 80,000 bottles a year of award-winning wine—four kinds of white, plus a sparkling "champagne." Upscale meals can be eaten indoors or on the beautiful vine-laden terrace with an outdoor fireplace. Sunday brunch is also served.

Take a tour ($4), sample the wine (free), or stroll the viticulturist trail, where panels explain wine making. (English translation available at the front desk.)

Most of the vineyards are wheelchair accessible.

SEASON AND HOURS
Regular business hours plus Sundays, all year.

FEES
Free. Tours $3.50–$4.50. Samples generally 50 cents (free at l'Orpailleur).

INFORMATION
Les Arpents de Neige (514) 295-3383;
Les Trois Clochers (514) 295-2034;
Les Côtes d'Ardoise (514) 295-2020;
Les Blancs Coteaux (514) 295-3503;
L'Orpailleur (514) 295-2763, in Montreal 341-1982. For a pamphlet listing two dozen vineyards in the Eastern Townships, call Tourisme Québec at 873-2015.

DIRECTIONS
Take Highway 10 (Eastern Townships Autoroute) east to exit 22. Follow Highway 35 south to Iberville, where it joins Route 133. Continue south on Route 133 to Pike River, then head east on Route 202 through Bedford, to the vineyards, just past Stanbridge East. To begin your tour at Les Arpents de Neige, continue past the vineyards to Dunham, and turn right at the junction. Les Arpents de Neige is 200 m along the road, on the right-hand side.

The Living Museum of Llamas (Llamadu) Mount Sutton

DRIVING TIME: 1 HR 20 MIN

One cold winter's night in 1991, Denise Machabee saw a classified ad for four llamas. Her family thought she was crazy, but pitched in to help when she bought them anyway. She now has 16 llamas (and counting), and the world has Llamadu, the Living Museum of Llamas. If you want to learn about these friendly, fascinating, and downy-soft creatures, spend a few hours at Llamadu. They'll soon win your hearts. You can even take one for a hike through the woods of Mount Sutton!

The tour starts at a picnic table, where Ms. Machabee presents a photo album showing llamas frolicking, courting, and giving birth. Kids will be fascinated, of course, but so will adults. Births are bloodless, for example, and in adaptation to their native Andean climate, llamas are always born before noon: if they don't make it one day, labour stops until the next.

Next you enter a corral full of llamas of all ages. As Ms. Machabee talks about their social lives and characteristics, curious llamas sneak up behind to sniff your collar or ear, because they recognize other llamas—and people, too—by their smell. They are very gentle and quiet, and make little chortling noises like a backed-up sink.

An informative and entertaining 16-min slide show (in English or French) is especially designed for children. It begins with volcanoes and dinosaurs, and culminates in the ancient llama.

It presents some interesting facts. Llamas have been around for 40 million years, and have been domesticated for 5,000–6,000. They are distant relatives of the camel (3.8-million-year-old llama-camel fossils have been found in California), but lack humps and require water every day. In South America, llamas are raised as pack animals and for their lanolin-free wool, collected by brushing, not shearing. Llamas also make good "guard dogs" in flocks of sheep.

As you may have heard, llamas spit. But don't worry, they only do it to each other. Females spit on males as part of the courtship ritual, and males, called "machos," spit on one another, just to show how tough they are.

When you leave the barn, you'll find a llama awaiting you. After a quick rundown on the llama-do's and llama-don'ts, you get to take one for a 600-, 800-, or 2,000-m walk in the woods on one of three trails. For longer hikes, you can rent a llama. They can even carry your pack up Mount Sutton for you.

I went with Jason, a very well behaved snow white llama. Like all llamas, he followed behind, and the lead was always slack. It was a very Zen experience, strolling through the hillside woods, across a couple of small footbridges, with a singing llama in tow. (Some llamas sing—hum, really—a lot.)

Other attractions at Llamadu include pheasants, quail, and turkeys. There's an angora goat named Pavarotti, who is very friendly and loves to be petted. There's also a very rare "wild llama," one of only seven on the continent. They are a protected species, so it is illegal to buy or sell them or to use their wool.

On the last weekend in July, Llamadu has a Sun Festival with Andean musicians.

SEASON AND HOURS
Every day, all year (closes briefly in early winter).

FEES
Adults $7, youth 7–13 $6, children 5–12 $3, under 5 free.
Llama rental: $15 per hour.

INFORMATION
Llamadu (514) 538-5521;
Eastern Townships Tourist Association (800) 355-5755.

DIRECTIONS
Take Highway 10 (Eastern Townships Autoroute) to exit 68. Follow Route 139 south. Just south of Sutton on Route 139, turn west on Jordan Rd. Llamadu is 5 km farther, on the right-hand side. For a more scenic drive, take exit 90 (Waterloo–Knowlton–Lac Brome) and follow Route 243 along the shores of Brome Lake. Head west on Route 104, then south on Valley Rd or Route 139 to Sutton.

Brome County Fair
Near Brome

DRIVING TIME: 1 HR

Photo: Joe Singerman

Autumn is the time for those who live off the land to relax and celebrate at the end of a long season of hard work. County fairs are traditional at this time of year, and the Brome County Fair is a shining example. It's Quebec's last of the season, but certainly not the least. During the four days it runs, you can take a gander at prize-winning livestock, enjoy country-style entertainment under the big tent, or simply join the crowds of merrymakers under the vast blue canopy of the Townships sky.

This old-style county fair is in no danger of losing its rural roots. There is animal judging every day, in the categories of dairy and beef cattle, sheep, swine, poultry, goats, and rabbits. An annual highlight is the harness racing on Monday afternoon, where pari-mutuel betting is strictly legal.

Other favourites are the horse pull, dance and music performances, and a petting zoo for children.

Two animal parades take place during the fair, generally on Sunday and Monday at 1 p.m. Sunday's is the largest livestock parade in the Eastern Townships. Over 300 animals are led through grounds and around the race-track by men, women, boys, and girls who hope to take home a blue ribbon. This event is best viewed from the grandstand.

Over 20 permanent buildings on the fairground house a variety of animals and exhibitions. Don't say nay to a stroll through the horse barn, where you can compare and contrast the many breeds and sizes. And the poultry house is something to crow about. It is a noisy, squawking place, with dozens of varieties of fowl from around the world, including colourful Chinese pheasants with extremely long tail feathers, snowwhite Chinese silkies with feathery feet and black beaks, and beautiful ducks. Delightful!

A building dedicated to the horticultural competition displays not just fruits and vegetables, but cut flowers, plants, home baking, canning, maple and honey products, and more, all vying for first prize. The handicraft competition gets a building of its own, too. Handmade items include knit and crocheted articles, quilts, paintings, and photographs. For those with an eye to purchase, there are stalls selling many crafts.

A fair wouldn't be a fair without junk food and a midway, and here, too, the Brome County Fair delivers. Concession stands and a cafeteria serve up snacks for all tastes, and the midway is large enough for variety, but small enough that you won't get lost. There are gentle rides to delight parents and children and others to shake the loose change from your pockets as you enjoy upside-down views of the surrounding countryside. Bonus! At the Brome County Fair all midway rides are included in the price of admission.

SEASON AND HOURS
Early to late, Fri–Mon, first weekend in Sept.

FEES
Adults $8, children under 12 $5.
Parking $3.

INFORMATION
(514) 242-EXPO (3976).

DIRECTIONS
Take Highway 10 (Eastern Townships Autoroute) to exit 74. Follow Pierre Laporte Blvd to Cowansville, then continue east on Route 104. From Brome, follow the temporary signs to the fairground.

Brome County
Historical Society Museum
Knowlton

DRIVING TIME: 1 HR 20 MIN

Photo: Brome County Historical Society Museum

The Brome County Historical Society Museum is a real surprise. Located a two-minute walk from the centre of laid-back Knowlton, the museum presents a rather plain exterior to the world. There are no neon signs flashing "This way!", but there ought to be. Inside this unassuming series of mixed-and-matched buildings is a wealth of treasures, including a penny-farthing bike, vintage clothing, a blacksmith shop, and oh yes, a full-size Fokker DVII biplane.

The War Room houses an impressive collection of World War I memorabilia, such as cloth posters with messages like "Your Chums Are Fighting, Why Aren't You?" and a pretty woman in a sailor's outfit saying "Gee, I wish I were a man, I'd join the Army." There is even the silhouette of a Commonwealth soldier used, not as target practice, but to fool the enemy.

The collection also includes a brass helmet of the Prussian Imperial Guard, with a 15-cm brass eagle on top, and a wooden canteen from the War of 1812.

The centrepiece is without a doubt the Fokker DVII biplane, the type piloted by the fabled Red Baron. This is an extremely rare and precious plane, the only one in North America (the one in the Smithsonian is a replica), and one of only three in the world. It was acquired when the German forces had to give up all their Fokkers under the Treaty of Versailles. The planes featured advanced technology permitting guns to be mounted behind the propeller; Commonwealth guns were mounted on the top wing, so aiming was more difficult, jammed guns couldn't be cleared, etc. And by the

72 Get Outta Town!

way, unlike the baron's plane, this one is painted in green camouflage.

Town founder Paul Knowlton believed in education, and the high school he built was no one-room schoolhouse. It was a two-storey building styled after upscale academies in England. It is on the museum grounds, and houses another part of the collection. Noteworthy architectural details include an interesting hand-painted ceiling border, a frieze patterned in a stylized floral motif.

Part of the ground floor retains its schoolhouse look, but much has been turned over to display cases. This room features a number of Indian artifacts, including baskets and comb cases intricately decorated with porcupine quills. There is also a mysterious long stone club. Unearthed locally in 1845, it was found 5 m below ground.

The upstairs has been remodelled in the style of a middle-class Victorian house typical of the Townships. It features a tip-top table dating from 1675 that functioned as a table, chair, and storage chest in the days when one room served many purposes. Also on display is a hair wreath. Before photographs, families made ornate floral wreaths from snippets of their loved ones' hair. Faded now, they must have looked quite lovely when new.

Collectors of Canadian first achievements will enjoy the radio room honouring Reginald Fessendon. Knowlton-born Fessendon (not Marconi), was the first to send a voice transmission over the airwaves. It was on Christmas Eve, 1906, from Brant Rock, Massachusetts, and was picked up by Morse-code receivers on ships at sea.

The volunteers of this oldest ongoing historical society in the province (founded 1898) and the inhabitants of Brome County, who have donated the entire collection, have done a terrific job of preserving Canadian and world history. The collection is important, interesting, and very approachable. On a rainy day, or even a sunny one, you'll enjoy the Brome County Historical Society Museum.

SEASON AND HOURS
10 a.m.–4:30 p.m., every day, mid-May–mid-Sept.

FEES
Adults $3, children and students $1.50, seniors $2.

INFORMATION
Museum (514) 243-6782;
Knowlton Tourist Bureau (514) 242-2870.

DIRECTIONS
Take Highway 10 (Eastern Townships Autoroute) to exit 90 (Waterloo–Knowlton–Lac Brome). Follow Route 243 south to Knowlton. The museum is just before the main intersection.

Gregorian Chanting at
St Benoît du Lac Abbey
Near Magog

DRIVING TIME: 1 HR 30 MIN

Photo: Eastern Townships Tourist Association

Lake Memphremagog is long and narrow, stretching 45 km from north to south. At the north end is Magog, a town busy with skiers in winter, and boaters and cottagers in summer. A mere 20 km from the hustle and bustle of Magog, but worlds apart, is the St Benoît du Lac abbey, nestled in the land that rolls gently through field and forest down to the lake's western shore.

Most of the monastery is closed to visitors, but twice a day the very modern chuch is open to the public (proper attire required). You can feast your eyes on the splendours of the architecture while basking your soul in the beauty of the Gregorian chanting that makes up a large part of each service and for which these Benedictine monks are famous.

The abbey was founded in 1912 by Dom Paul Vannier after the Benedictines were expelled from Normandy, France, at the turn of the century. About 60 monks now live there, devoting themselves to prayer, work, and helping those in need, according to the rule set down by St Benedict (circa 480–547) (Benoît in French).

The recently completed church was designed by Montreal architect Dan Hanganu. Montrealers will be familiar with his work, since Hanganu also designed the Université de Montréal's École des Hautes Études Commerciales and the Pointe à Callière Museum in the Old Port.

A long connecting hall leads from the entrance of the abbey to the doors of the church. The hall is flooded with natural sunlight, and the floor is a colourful mosaic of white, black, yellow, green, blue, red, and tan bricks. At the doors to the church is a shallow stainless-steel basin set on a modern pedestal. The basin is lit by a halogen spotlight suspended from the wall by a 3-m stainless-steel rod that projects through the transom and into the church.

The nave is perfectly symmetrical, with walls of warmly coloured tan brick, punctuated by lines of red. The upper gallery features a series of crenellated arches. According to Hanganu, the missing bricks in the arches represent the Benedictine monks "stepping back, removing themselves, to make a difference."

On bright afternoons, the sun shines through the windows beyond the altar. Fifteen-metre stainless-steel cables suspended from the ceiling just in front cast geometric shadows on the floor. The interior is highlighted by the exposed steel structure of the building.

This is the modern yet monastic atmosphere in which services are held. Visitors are welcome to attend—and are bound to be impressed. Some of the monks wear black robes, others white. The chanting takes place mainly from the choir, but at times a group of monks gather in front of the first simple wooden pews. The acoustics are superb, and the haunting beauty of a live performance is unforgettable.

Downstairs from the entrance is the abbey gift shop, where you can purchase cider and cheese made on the premises, religious articles, and tapes of Gregorian chanting. If the boutique is closed when you are there, the general store in Austin carries the cider and cheese at the same prices.

Also on the grounds is a guesthouse where men can withdraw for a few days in an atmosphere of peace and meditation. Women are welcomed in the nearby Villa St Scholastique, a retreat run by nuns.

SEASON AND HOURS
All year. Eucharist celebrated daily 11 a.m. and Vespers 5 p.m. (7 p.m. Thursdays). Both services feature Gregorian chants. Boutique: Every day except Sunday, 9:00 a.m.–10:45 a.m. and 2:00 p.m.–4:30 p.m.

FEES
Donations accepted.

INFORMATION
(819) 843-4080.

DIRECTIONS
Take the Champlain Bridge and follow Highway 10 (Eastern Townships Autoroute) to exit 115 (Mont Orford–Magog). Follow Route 112 east to Chemin des Pères. Go south on Chemin des Pères to Austin. At Austin, follow the signs to the monastary, heading towards the lake.

Circuit des Arts
Memphrémagog (Art Tour)
Magog Area
DRIVING TIME: VARIES (1 HR 15 MIN TO MAGOG)

Each summer, over 100 artists and artisans in the region of Lake Memphremagog open the doors of their homes, galleries, and studios to visitors. The Memphremagog Art Tour is a great chance to see a wide variety of works, mainly in the visual arts, and to meet the people who created them. And you don't have to be an art expert to appreciate the beauty of the Townships countryside!

The third annual art tour (1996) involved 105 artists at 62 locations from rural Highwater (near Mansonville) to exurban North Hatley, with the vast majority in Magog and around Lake Memphremagog. Each year, an easy-to-read map is issued, indicating the participants and their media. Numbered temporary signs posted on the road make it a snap to find a particular artist.

Route 247 rolls along the western shores of Lake Memphremagog, through farmland and forest, offering occasional views of the lake itself. The art tour map listed 10 stops along the road between Magog and Georgeville, where you could view photography, stoneware, water colours and oils, jewellery, sculpture, and more. This particular itinerary also included some decidedly interesting architecture.

Oil painter Marcel Poirier lives in a modern development of large houses on even larger lakeside lots. He has turned his yard into a living work of art. A fieldstone path leads from the road, alongside the pond he built, and to his studio. A number of totem poles and sculptures decorate the path and yard—indicating the energy of this self-taught artist.

Mr. Poirier's large, brightly coloured canvases illustrate scenes of Montreal, New York, and the tropics. Despite the facelessness of the people in his paintings, the canvases are incredibly engaging, and speak warmly of an urban and village community spirit.

A few kilometres south, John Di Nezza, head of the volunteer group that organizes the circuit, has set up shop in another architectural delight. His photo studio and exhibition space are in a barn that once housed 13,000 chickens. Di Nezza's infrared Townships landscapes are mesmerising.

Jason Krpan, of Georgeville, is a well-known poet and maker of stoneware pottery. His home is another living sculpture. Mr. Krpan fishes cedar driftwood out of the lake and plants it upside down around his home and garden. He calls his home "Cedar Heaven" and the trees "born-again cedars." The locals call them dragons, because of the serpentine look of their twisted, water-polished roots. To one side of his house is a large vegetable garden, in a series of concentric circles, with a teepee structure for climbing beans in its centre. You'll recognize Mr. Krpan's house from the road by the giant concrete turtle on top of the chimney.

Georgeville's famous Elephant Barn has never housed 13,000 elephants, but it does have a dancing elephant painted on one of its bright red walls. It is also well known as an art centre, offering a variety of courses all summer long. During the art tour, a dozen sculptors, painters, jewellers, and other artists and artisans display their creations, some of them of exceptional quality. There is usually an artist at work.

To plan your tour, call for the location of the map outlet nearest you, or simply head out to Magog and pick up a map at the tourist office or at your first stop.

SEASON AND HOURS (1996)
10 a.m.–5 p.m., daily, Jul 27–Aug 4.
FEES
Free.
INFORMATION
Magog–Orford Tourist Office
(800) 267-2744, (819) 843-2744.
DIRECTIONS
Take the Champlain Bridge and follow Highway 10 (Eastern Townships Autoroute) to exit 115 (Mont Orford–Magog). Follow Route 112 east into Magog. The tourist office is on Route 112, at the head of the lake.

Montreal, Laval, and

The main focus of this book is trips into the countryside, but it would be a mistake to overlook some of the terrific destinations in the immediate

Photo: David Inglis

area. Not only are many of them accessible by public transit, they are every bit as lovely as their rural counterparts. You'll be pleasantly surprised to discover how easily you can get that out-of-town feeling, right here on the island.

This section features strolls through the two last virgin forests on the island—in the Morgan Arboretum and the Bois de Liesse Nature Park—as well as a visit to the only remaining marshland, in the Pointe aux Prairies Nature Park.

the South Shore

In addition, this section covers two destinations in Laval (Île Jésus): the Cosmodome and the Laval Nature Centre. It also includes two—the Marsil Museum and the Canadian Railway Museum—on the South Shore. Strictly speaking, the museums should be in the Montérégie section, but they are so close, they are included here. Due to limited space, directions by public transit could not be given. Please contact the destinations themselves for information.

Photo: Estelle Bolker

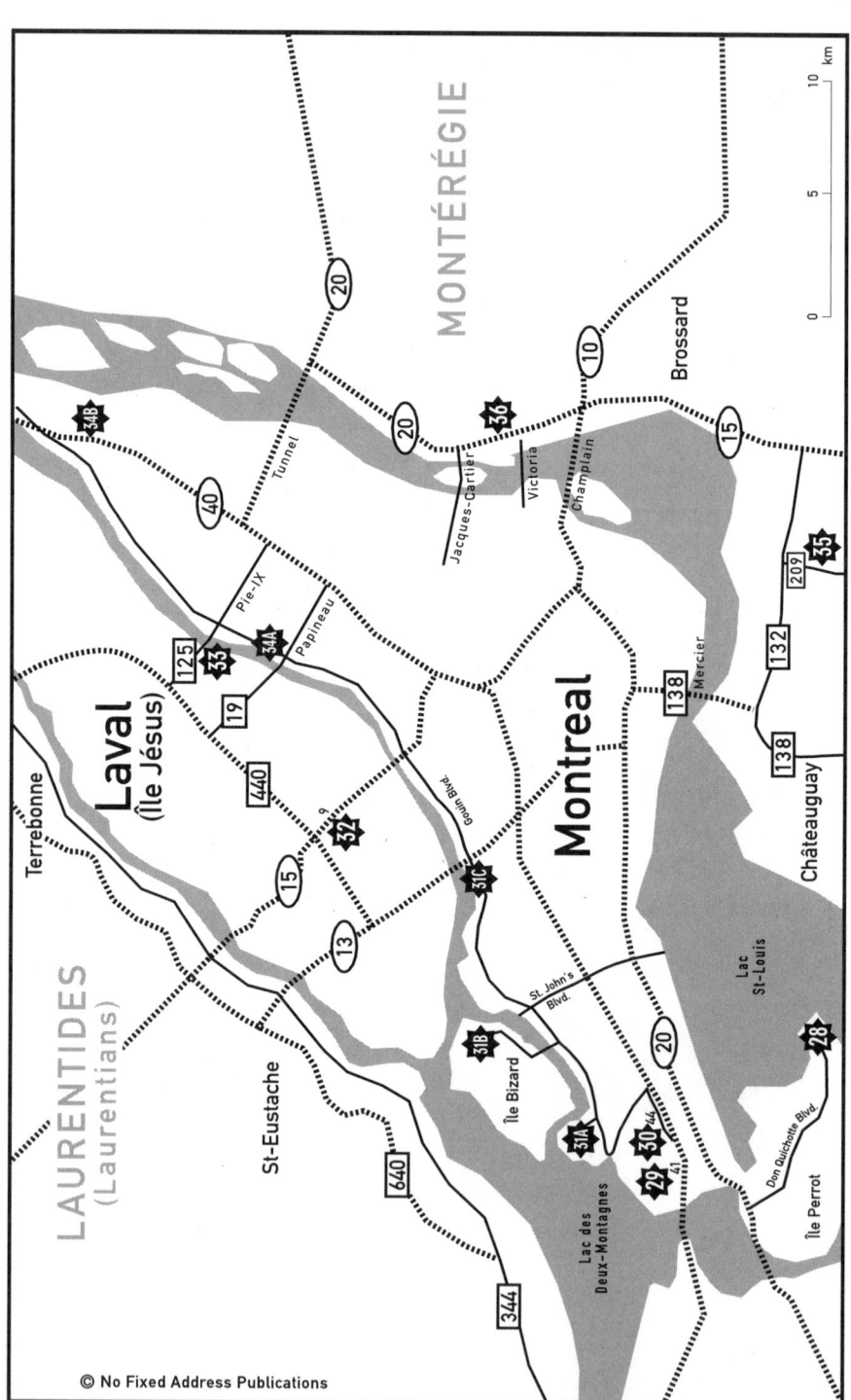

MONTREAL, LAVAL, & SOUTH SHORE

Trip Destinations

28 Pointe du Moulin
Île Perrot
(514) 453-5936
p.82

29 Morgan Arboretum
St Anne de Bellevue
(514) 398-7812
p.84

30 Ecomuseum
St Anne de Bellevue
(514) 457-9449
p.86

31A Cap St Jacques Nature Park
Pierrefonds
Chalet: (514) 280-6871;
Eco-Farm: (514) 280-6743
p.88

31B Bois de l'Île Bizard Nature Park
Île Bizard
(514) 280-8517
p.88

31C Bois de Liesse Nature Park
Pierrefonds/Dollard des Ormeaux
(514) 280-6720, (514) 280-6678
p.88

32 Cosmodome, Laval
(514) 978-3600
p.90

33 Laval Nature Centre
Laval
(514) 662-4942
p.92

34A Île de la Visitation Nature Park
Ahunsic
(514) 280-6733
p.94

34B Pointe aux Prairies Nature Park
Rivière des Prairies/
Pointe aux Trembles
(514) 280-6691
p.94

35 Canadian Railway Museum
Delson/St Constant
(514) 632-2410
p.96

36 Marsil Museum of Clothing,
Textiles, and Fibre
St Lambert
(514) 671-3098.
p.98

Tourist Information

Tourisme Québec Infotourist Centre
(514) 873-2015, (800) 363-7777

Greater Montreal Convention and
Tourist Bureau
(514) 844-5400, (800) 363-7777

Laval Maison du Tourisme
(514) 682-5522, (800) 463-3765

Montreal Urban Community Transit
Corporation (MUCTC)
(514) AUTO-BUS (288-6287)

Île Perrot (seasonal)
(514) 587-5750

Tilting at Windmills at
Pointe du Moulin
Île Perrot
DRIVING TIME: 35 MIN

You know you're on the way to Windmill Point when you turn onto Don Quichotte (Don Quixote) Blvd. Once past the surfeit of car dealerships, it is easy enough to imagine a donkey-riding knight clip-clopping along this lovely country road to the windmill. The delightful little park on the southern tip of the island has walking paths, two picnic areas, a visitor's centre, and, of course, an old windmill.

As you enter the park, you pass through one of the nicest visitor's centres to be found. The wood-shingled buildings are an architectural surprise—they appear to have been been divided in half and separated to make way for the path. Inside are a snack bar, toilets, and a water cooler. You might want to fill up before venturing out into the park, since water is not always available further along.

There is a small exhibtion on early farming practices, and children can dip their hands into buckets of wheat, barley, oats, and buckwheat.

A scale model of the windmill's inner works occupies a large part of one room. Children will enjoy tossing in sandbags that look like grain. Next, a staff member turns on the windmill, and out comes "flour." Finally, kids can sift the ground grain to separate the larger bits from the smaller.

A short walk through some very nice woods—there is also a trail with panels explaining plants and animals of interest—leads to a shaded point of land with a grassy area. The miller's house is worth a visit, especially on Sunday afternoons, when bread is baked the old-fashioned way in a wood-fired brick oven. Samples are served.

Right next door is the windmill, dating from 1708. It is one of two still operational in the province of Quebec (the other is on Île aux Coudres, near Quebec City). Due to the age of the windmill, its sails aren't set in motion too often—the wind has to be just right—and it is only on the occasional Sunday that you will see it working.

Working or not, it is a remarkable construction. The roof is a heavy wooden structure weighing about 5 t. Despite its weight, it can be rotated so that the sails will pick up the wind. This is why, like most windmills, it has two doors—it allows the miller a means of entering and exiting no matter which side the sails are on. As a note of interest, when a miller forgot and left through the wrong door, the windmill was dubbed a *"moulin rouge"* (red windmill) after the unfortunate accident that ensued.

Also noteworthy are the rectangular holes in the windmill's walls, a couple of metres off the ground. While it appears as if bricks or floor beams have fallen out, in reality these are loopholes, through which weapons could be fired.

Defending a mill may seem a bit odd, but there is some question as to whether the windmill ever actually ground much grain. Seigneur Perrot, the rumour goes, was actually a big dealer in the illegal fur trade, intercepting canoes on their way to Montreal, both by bribe and by force. This earned him enemies on both sides of the trading counter, and resulted in what may be the world's only defendable windmill. Tilt your lance at that one, Don Quixote.

SEASON AND HOURS
9 a.m.–6 p.m., every day, mid-May–Aug; 12 p.m.–6 p.m., weekends and holidays, Sept–Thanksgiving.

FEES
Free.

INFORMATION
(514) 453-5936.

DIRECTIONS
Take Highway 20 west to Île Perrot. Once on the island, turn south on Don Quichotte Blvd and follow it to the end.

Year-Round Beauty at the
Morgan Arboretum
St Anne de Bellevue

DRIVING TIME: 30 MIN

In the late 19th century, retailing mogul James Morgan of Morgan's department store fame (now The Bay) consolidated 21 farm lots straddling St Anne de Bellevue and Senneville, on the western tip of the island. On weekends, friends of the family would take the train to St Anne's, then picnic or ride on 245 ha of pristine fields and woodlands. The trains are gone, and horses rarely seen, but Canada's largest arboretum lives on, and it is open to visitors all year long.

Since its acquisition by McGill University in 1945—partly purchased by the university and partly donated by the Morgan family—the arboretum has been dedicated to the preservation of trees and shrubs (*arbor* is Latin for tree). In fact, the arboretum was the first tree farm in Quebec, certified in 1953. For over 50 years, staff and volunteers have been planting and tending, with remarkable results. The area now boasts 150 species of trees and shrubs and over 350 species of smaller plants.

It is not just the variety of growth, but the way it is laid out, that makes a walk through the arboretum a treat, any time of year. As you stroll the wide, well-maintained paths, you pass through 20 separate collections of trees. One moment, you're in an apple orchard, the next, an open field. A few steps later, you'll pass by row upon row of birch trees. An especially interesting stretch is the spruce, cedar, and juniper forest set in a glen. In gardens, these trees are usually neatly trimmed; here, they have an untamed look, like a topiary garden gone wild. Many trees are clearly identified.

The arboretum's maple stands, with trees over 200 years old, are some of Montreal's last remaining virgin forest; the Bois de Liesse Nature Park has the only other uncut woods on the island. There is also plenty of secondary growth, well over a century old.

In the warm season, something is always blooming: apple trees or rose bushes, magnolias or lilacs, or simply wildflowers in fields. For picnickers, there are tables near the conservation centre, which has toilets and a snack bar.

For a self-guided tour, pick up a booklet and make tracks. Two Forest Management trails (1.2 km and 1.8 km) offer interesting insights into the forces that affect a forest's growth. The Ecology Trail (2 km) brings you closer to the ferns and microhabitats of one of the wetter parts of the arboretum.

In winter, the arboretum keeps 20 km of trails open for use, including 7 km of groomed cross-country ski trails (mainly easy). A kilometre and a half of the central road is kept ploughed for walking.

The arboretum hosts a number of special weekends throughout the year. In mid-December the conservation centre turns into a gift shop for a day, selling high-quality locally made crafts. Christmas trees are also sold throughout the month.

In early March, Springfest features a whole host of activities for all ages. The prize-winning Macdonald Woodsmen put on a show that includes cross-cut sawing, bow sawing, horizontal and vertical chopping, and axe throwing. In the afternoon, children are invited to participate in friendly, safe young woodsman competitions.

Keep an eye out for the sugaring-off open house later in March. Watch the sap boil or feast on *tourtière* (meat pie), baked beans, and other traditional fare.

SEASON AND HOURS
10:30 a.m.–4 p.m., every day, all year. Members only on winter weekends.

FEES
Adults $4, children $2, under 5 free.

INFORMATION
(514) 398-7812.

DIRECTIONS
Take Highway 40 (Trans-Canada) west to exit 41 (St Anne de Bellevue). Continue on St Marie Rd. Turn left on Chemin des Pins (Pine Rd).

Caribou and Timber Wolves at the Ecomuseum
St Anne de Bellevue

DRIVING TIME: 30 MIN

Photo: Estelle Bolker

The Ecomuseum is Montreal's own "Field of Dreams." In 1965, McGill University's Roger Bider visited the Arizona Sierra Museum, where desert wildlife resides in ecologically designed enclosures, the goal of which is to encourage preservation of the animals' natural habitats. The idea stayed with him, and in the early, 80s he began shifting earth on an old landfill and dump on the West Island. He got a helping hand when, as soon as the first enclosure was built, a man brought him two orphaned bear cubs. What could he do? He offered the bears a home. Dr Bider built it, and they came.

The bears are still there, and they've been joined by caribou, wolves, arctic foxes, raccoons, skunks, porcupines, coyotes, otters, deer, lynx, snakes, turtles—the list is impressive. The Ecomuseum has succeeded in its goal of representing the major species of wildlife native to the St Lawrence Valley. It has over 40 species in all, housed in almost two dozen environments, nicely arranged along comfortable walking paths.

The Ecomuseum is a wildlife observation centre, not a zoo: the key difference lies in its educational role. That said, it's too bad more zoos aren't like the Ecomuseum. Most of the enclosures are large and were designed with the needs of the animals in mind. In addition, the animals are allowed to follow their natural rhythms. If you visit in winter, for example, you won't see the bears, because they'll be hibernating. And while porcupines and raccoons don't hibernate, they do hide out during the colder months. No attempt is made to convince them to do otherwise.

One highlight is the walk-in aviary. Over 14 species of waterfowl and other birds fly freely under a huge net canopy. A boardwalk leads through various habitats, including a marshy area where some birds nest and a pretty stand of sumac and cedar. The raven and crow enclosure always draws a crowd. These clever birds are real talkers and seem to love human attention.

Wolves used to be common in the St Lawrence Valley, and the Ecomuseum has two beautiful animals. The male is larger and is pure timber wolf. The female is of mixed breed—part timber wolf, Siberian wolf, and dog.

The Ecomuseum also has an impressive assortment of birds of prey, acquired when it absorbed part of the McGill raptor centre. These are injured birds that could not survive in the wild. Most of them sit on top of their doghouse-style homes, tethered to a wire that allows them to fly to a perch.

One habitat often overlooked—probably due to its bunker-like entrance—is the experimental fish pond. It's worth the trip down the damp concrete staircase for a mud-puppy's-eye view of life in a pond. This pond is left to its own devices, so actually seeing any fish can be a challenge. In winter, the algae die, so the water is much clearer.

There are two special events at the Ecomuseum. On Easter weekend, the staff hides hundreds of clothespegs, which can be traded in for chocolate eggs. On the last weekend in October, it's time for Chuck-a-Duck Day. Injured ducks are often brought to the museum to be nursed back to health and on this day you bid for the privilege of releasing one back into the wild.

SEASON AND HOURS
9 a.m.–5 p.m., every day, year round. (Closed Christmas and New Year's.)

FEES
Adults $4, children 5–12 (accompanied) $2, children 5–12 (school groups) $4, under 5 free.

INFORMATION
(514) 457-9449.

DIRECTIONS
Take Highway 40 (Trans-Canada) west to exit 44 (Morgan Blvd). Turn left at the stop sign and continue west on St Marie Rd to the Ecomuseum entrance, on the right-hand side.

MUC
Nature Parks
West Island

DRIVING TIME: 20–30 MIN (VARIES)

Bois de l'Île Bizard Nature Park has three entrances, but you'll do well to begin at the visitor's centre, where you'll find an information desk, as well as a snack bar and toilets. You can rent kayaks or canoes to explore the recreational side of the park, or bicycles for the conservation area.

The tiny beach at this park is never crowded, and its shallow water is ideal for a paddle with the kids. A grassy peninsula with a picnic area and a gazebo overlooking the lake and beach is a great place to take in the sunset, but don't forget the insect repellent.

The park's conservation area has a fantastic boardwalk stretching for 0.5 km over a large marsh and a number of paths leading through beech, cedar, and maple forests.

Cap St Jacques is the largest, most diverse, and most remote of the nature parks, bordered on three sides by water. It has 27 km of shared hiking and biking trails, a huge beach, and a working farm.

Packed-earth paths crisscrossing the maple forest are very popular with hikers in autumn, and even more popular with skiers in winter.

There are a multitude of grassy picnic areas, most with views of Lake of Two Mountains, all of them well maintained, with toilets and coal disposal for barbecues. The nicest is l'Embouchure (the mouth), a real gem overlooking the lake, the back river (Rivière des Prairies), and Oka in the distance.

The Eco-Farm is a full-size working farm with two barns and a greenhouse open to visitors. A gorgeous vegetable garden is set in wide arcs, and the horses, pigs, highland cows, chickens, angora goats and other animals are beautifully kept. There is also a restaurant and large picnic area here.

Cap St Jacques is well-known for its public beach on Lake of Two Mountains. Weekends, this popular beach turns into a mini-Cape Cod. The beach is a 1-km hike from the nearest parking lot, or you can take the shuttle train from the main parking lot for $1.25.

At 193 ha, **Bois de Liesse Nature Park** is about the size of Mount Royal. Like the others, it is very clean and well managed, with perfectly maintained cycling and hiking paths. It is organized into three distinct areas.

The path in the peninsula area follows Betrand Creek, one of the last open streams on the island. It has several nice lookouts, and you'll almost certainly see ducks, herons, and beaver lodges.

The fields area, inland, has nice wide paths edged with fieldstones. Some fields are mowed; others are left to themselves.

The Bois Franc area is the largest and most spectacular, with an extraordinary maple and beech stand. A wide log-edged path leads through a healthy forest carpeted with bright ferns. Some of the trees are over 100 years old. There is a Japanese-style boardwalk several feet off the wettest part of the forest floor. Take insect repellent!

SEASON AND HOURS
Parks: All year.
Chalets (Cap St Jacques): All year.
Chalets (others): mid-April–mid-Dec.

INFORMATION
Bois de l'Île Bizard: 280-8517.
Cap St Jacques: Chalet 280-6871, Eco-Farm 280-6743.
Bois de Liesse: 280-6720 or 280-6678.

DIRECTIONS
Bois de l'Île Bizard
From Highway 20 or Highway 40 (Trans-Canada), go north on St John's Blvd. Head west on Pierrefonds Blvd, then north on Jacques Bizard Blvd onto Île Bizard. On Île Bizard, turn right on Cherrier Rd, and follow it past the rapids and the ferry to Laval to the entrance.

Cap St Jacques
Take Highway 40 (Trans-Canada) west to exit (St Marie Rd). Follow St Marie west, then turn north on L'Anse a l'Orme Rd and keep going to Gouin Blvd. Head east on Gouin to the entrance.

Bois de Liesse
Take Highway 20 or Highway 40 (Trans-Canada) west to Highway 13. Follow Highway 13 north to Gouin Blvd. Follow signs to the entrance at 9432 Gouin Blvd West.

To Infinity and Beyond at the Cosmodome Laval

DRIVING TIME: 25 MIN

Photo: Laval Tourism Bureau

When you pass through the sliding doors of Laval's Cosmodome, you enter a world beyond time and space. The lighting is space-station subdued, and guides in NASA blue jumpsuits greet you at the door.

Though similar to Ottawa's Science Centre, the Cosmodome focusses exclusively on the history of aerospace, telecommunications, and computer science. Space noises, push buttons, holograms, and computer graphics abound in this museum, making it a blend of science centre, video game, and amusement park.

The museum features truly beautiful scale models of various missiles and rockets—including a full-size replica of the world's first satellite, *Sputnik*—as well as astronomically inspired historic sites such as Stonehenge and Mayan temples, with detailed explanations of the cosmological reasons behind their designs.

One area features a model of our own solar system, with a huge glowing demihemisphere of the sun on one wall. Each planet is to scale and is surrounded by a shallow well showing what its surface is believed to look like. Earth's has ferns growing in it, for example, while Venus's is charred by sulphuric acid. The wells of the four gas giants—Jupiter, Saturn, Uranus, and Neptune—feature dry-ice mist floating up from the base.

But while the size of the planets is to scale, the distance between them is not: if Montreal were the sun, Earth and Mars would be near Ottawa, Pluto would be in Vancouver, and Uranus would be somewhere near Winnipeg. A

90   Get Outta Town!

video screen by each planet presents the facts, and high-resolution computer animation simulates a trip across the planet's surface.

Sound doesn't travel in a vacuum, and at the Cosmodome they offer proof. One of the hands-on displays features a bell ringing inside a glass chamber. When you press a button, the air is sucked out of the chamber, and the ringing fades away.

Another display explains the nature of satellite communication. You speak into a parabolic dish. The sound travels through air upwards to another dish—the "satellite"—where it is carried by wire to another, then back down through air to the receiving parabolic dish.

Don't skip the superb 360-degree multimedia show that combines film, slides, holographic projections, and 3,500 optical fibres to present a history of human interest in the cosmos. While the acting is a little hokey, the show is informative, entertaining, and a technological wonder in itself. The holographic projections are so real you can almost feel the flames as the library of Alexandria burns. In another scene, Newton dances gleefully while apples swarm around him like planets. It's difficult to determine what's real and what isn't, as the 100-seat theatre tilts, rotates, rises, and descends to various scenes, with incredible *trompe l'oeil* sets.

The Cosmodome also runs a space camp, which is open to the public several times a year. You'll get the chance to be tossed and turned by seven simulators demonstrating various principles of space travel. The "multiaxis" is like a multidimensional lettuce dryer. The space wall, where you try to open doors and undo bolts while strapped into a chair that simulates weightlessness, is a refreshingly sedate experience in comparison.

By the way, the rocket ship out front is a three-quarter scale replica of the *Ariane IV*, the European satellite launcher that made its debut in 1988. The *Ariane* series has launched several Canadian satellites, including the *Anik E2* in 1991. At 46 m, the replica is as tall as a 15-storey building.

SEASON AND HOURS
9 a.m.–5 p.m., Tues–Sun, all year.

FEES
Adults $9.50, students $7.50, seniors and youth 13–22 $6.50, children 6–12 $6.50.

INFORMATION
978-3600.

DIRECTIONS
Take Highway 15 (Laurentian Autoroute) north to exit 9 (St Martin Blvd. West). From there, follow the signs 3 km to the entrance.

Four-Season, All-Weather Fun at the Laval
Nature Centre
Laval
DRIVING TIME: 40 MIN

It's a mystery how the Laval Nature Centre has managed to remain unknown to so many Montrealers. This well-established park has been in existence for over 20 years, receives over a million visitors annually, and offers a variety of things to do, especially for families, all year round. Farm animals, deer, a tropical greenhouse, plus the biggest and best outdoor skating rink around—what more could you want in a park? Not only is it easy to get to by car, everything, including admission and parking, is free.

The nature centre is in located in an old quarry on the south edge of Île Jésus, just west of the Pie IX Bridge. Though thoroughly landscaped, the quarry is still discernible in the cliffs that plunge straight into the large artificial lake that was once the main pit.

Children will enjoy a stroll through the small, modern, clean barn, just on the other side of the lake from the main entrance. It houses a number of animals, including a cow, a horse, some pheasants, a huge pig that tips the scales at over 300 kg—even a farm cat and a couple of mice. Part of the barn has been turned into an indoor duck pond, with a bridge over it for viewing.

Next door is a greenhouse full of tropical plants and exotic birds, both caged and flying loose. The Japanese carp in the fast-flowing pool are actually part of the school at the Botanical Gardens. This is a co-operative safety precaution between the two installations; if the fish at one park die of disease, there will be others available for restocking. These beautiful creatures can cost upwards of several thousand dollars apiece—so no fishing!

Just up a hill from the barn and greenhouse is another surprise, a large chain-link enclosure with nine white-tailed deer.

All the facilities are open in winter, when the park turns into a hub of outdoor activity. To 3 km of cleared walking paths, the centre adds 7 km groomed for cross-country skiing and skate-skiing. There is a small hill with several slopes for tobogganing, too, but the *pièce de résistance* is the giant skating rink on the artificial lake. It covers an area about the size of 18 hockey rinks. Call ahead for ice conditions, since the lake is very deep and consequently the ice takes some time to freeze. The park management claims it's the best outdoor ice in Quebec, and there's little reason to doubt it: the lake is cleared and maintained using a Zamboni machine! (The Bonsecour Basin in Old Montreal is the only other outdoor rink to Zamboni its ice.)

You can rent skates, have yours sharpened, or just stop in for a snack and some hot chocolate in the lakeside chalet.

Both winter and summer, the centre provides an extraordinary amount of free family entertainment (in French only). On most weekends, and weekdays during school holidays, there are special activities ranging from treasure hunts to dogsledding. Over 70,000 people gathered in the park for family fun and an outdoor concert last St Jean Baptiste Day (June 24).

SEASON AND HOURS
Chalet and other buildings: 9 a.m.–10 p.m.

FEES
Free admission and parking.

INFORMATION
(514) 662-4942.

DIRECTIONS
Take Highway 15 (Laurentian Autoroute) north to Highway 440 (Laval Autoroute). Take the 440 east to Highway 19 (Papineau Autoroute), then follow Highway 19 south (towards Montreal) to exit 5 (Concorde Blvd). Follow Concorde Blvd east to Avenue du Parc. The park is bordered by Concorde Blvd to the south, St Martin Blvd to the north, and Highway 25 to the east. The main entrance is on Avenue du Parc. Accessible by public transport; call the park for directions.

MUC
Nature Parks
East End

DRIVING TIME: 20-30 MIN

Ile de la Visitation Nature Park is the smallest of the MUC nature parks, occupying only 33 ha, but it is the most popular. This little island paradise on the edge of the Rivière des Prairies, in the 300-year-old district of Ahuntsic, has all the ingredients for a pleasant outing not too far from home: history, natural beauty, and great views.

From the visitor's centre you can walk a circuit that takes you onto the island, along wooded paths, and back to the mainland over the ruins of an old mill. In all, the park has 2.5 km of paths for biking, 6.9 km for walking, and three picnic areas (though the only toilets are in the visitor's centre).

A children's exhibition (in French only) at the Maison du Pressoir presents the early history of the area, when Ahuntsic was a small village isolated from Montreal. A highlight is the full-sized apple press from which the house derives its name. Here you can pick up a pamphlet (also in French only) for a self-guided walking tour of 25 historic houses in the district. The nearby Église de la Visitation is a good example of the architectural treasures in this area. Built in 1752, it is the oldest church in Montreal.

In 1928, the island was levelled during construction of the hydro dam off its eastern tip. As a result, the growth is almost all new, and each year the park's staff adds more flowering trees and bushes. There is a nice gazebo overlooking the dam and a mossy overflow wall. You're bound to see ducks or herons here, and there are almost always people fishing. (Unfortunately, there is no boating or windsurfing, since the water level can fluctuate by several metres in just a few hours.)

Pointe aux Prairies Nature Park, located just about where Sherbrooke St and Gouin Blvd meet, straddles both the back river (Rivière des Prairies) and the St Lawrence. It has 13.5 km of hiking and cycling trails, with 3 km for hiking only. This park has several nice picnic areas and three visitor's centres.

The back river area is in many ways the loveliest part of the park. The only marshland on the Island of Montreal is here, teeming with waterfowl. A wooden walkway crosses a portion of the marsh, and there is a covered platform where you can picnic. The visitor's centre features a stone observation tower, and a high-tech windmill keeps up the water level in the marsh.

A narrow strip of land connects the north edge of the park to the centre, winding by the MUC sewage treatment centre and under Highway 40. This may sound like an unpleasant walk, but it isn't—though the path is somewhat shadeless and exposed.

South of the highway, a narrow trail leads through old-growth Laurentian forest, mainly a mix of birch and maple. The unmanaged woods at the park's southern limits are just that—a rather rough trail leading to the St Lawrence, suitable for hikers and mountain bikers. In wet weather, it can get quite muddy underfoot.

Île de la Visitation

SEASON AND HOURS
April 26–Labour Day:
10:00 a.m.–7:00 p.m.
Labour Day–Oct 26: 9:30 a.m.–4:30 p.m.
Dec 14–March 15: 9:30 a.m.–4:30 p.m.

FEES
Free.

INFORMATION
280-6733.

DIRECTIONS
Take Highway 40 (Metropolitan Expressway) east to the Papineau exit. Follow Papineau north to Henri Bourassa. Head east on Henri Bourassa. At the third light, turn north on De l'Île. Go east on Gouin Blvd 200m to the park entrance (on the left).

Pointe aux Prairies

SEASON AND HOURS
April 26–mid-October:
11:00 a.m.–5:00 p.m.

FEES
Free.

INFORMATION
280-6691.

DIRECTIONS
Take Highway 40 (Metropolitan Expressway) east to exit 85 (St Jean Baptiste Blvd). Turn north on St Jean Baptiste Blvd to Gouin Blvd. Head east on Gouin to either of two entrances (14905 and 12300 Gouin East).

Canadian Railway Museum
St Constant
DRIVING TIME: 30 MIN

Take a trolley into the past, ride a diesel train, or send a message by telegraph. Those are just some of the things you can do at the Canadian Railway Museum, where you could spend a good portion of the day inspecting the firsts, lasts, biggests, and smallests of the engines and rolling stock that built and united our nation. The museum has examples of just about everything that ever set wheel to rail: locomotives, cabooses, passenger cars, trolleys—over 120 in all. The expansive grounds are anything but crowded, and since there are two large sheds, the railway museum is good fun even on a rainy day.

Youngsters will be thrilled and oldsters will feel nostalgic as they shake, rattle, and roll on the streetcar that used to run along St Catherine Street. When the city took the last streetcars out of service, it hauled all 200 into a north-end field to be burned. At the last minute, this particular one was rescued, for sentimental reasons, because its number was 1959—the year of Montreal's last streetcar.

Another exhibit is the world's first pay-as-you-enter streetcar, which made its debut in Montreal in 1925. And then there's the school car, an invention that remained uniquely Canadian. From 1927 to 1967, specially built cars like this one served the railway towns of northern Ontario. The two cars of each teaching train contained a kitchen, living area, and a classroom with 15 desks. (When a community had 16 school-age children, they could build a schoolhouse.) The cars stayed put for lessons, but moved from place to place on a weekly basis—kids were taught just one week of each month.

The *Dominion of Canada*, dating from 1937, is aerodynamic and brightly painted—unusual for a sooty steam engine. It was designed for speed, and in 1939 it broke the world record for a train when it clocked over 200 km/h. That's Montreal to Toronto in two and a half hours! Kids will get a kick out of the "secret passage" alongside the boiler. Rumour has it that if you're quiet, you might hear the ghost that's said to live inside.

Another special sight is the *Golden Chariot*, an open-air streetcar with tiers of ornate seats, gilt ironwork and pastel yellow wood. In the days when seven tickets cost a quarter, the *Golden Chariot* offered a luxury tour of Montreal's Westmount and Mount Royal peaks for 50 cents.

An exhibit that is breathtaking in its proportions is the *Selkirk 5935*. It was built in 1949, when steam engines were rapidly being replaced by the cleaner diesel-electrics. The Canadian Pacific Railway wanted the biggest steam engine in the world. At 5 m tall, 10 m long, and 365 t, they almost got it. The *Selkirk* is gargantuan.

Huffing and puffing demonstrations of the *John Molson*, a black, red, and brass "choo-choo train"—a replica of an original built in 1849—are regularly scheduled on Sundays throughout the summer. The demonstrations are in the early afternoon, but the staff starts stoking the fire in the morning: it takes four hours to build the head of steam needed to put the engine into locomotion.

On Sundays you can also ride a diesel train, or send a real telegram from Barrington Station, an authentic country station built in 1882.

SEASON AND HOURS
9 a.m.–5 p.m., mid-May–Labour Day.

FEES
Adults $5.25, students and seniors $4.25, children 5–12 $2.75, children under 4 free. Cheaper during the week. Family rates available.

INFORMATION
(514) 632-2410.

DIRECTIONS
Go over the Mercier Bridge, take the La Prairie exit, then head east on Route 132. At the 5th traffic light, turn right onto Route 209 south. The museum is just before the train tracks, on the left-hand side.

Marsil Museum
of Clothing, Textiles, and Fibre
St Lambert

DRIVING TIME: 20 MIN

The Marsil Museum of Clothing, Textiles, and Fibre has a name that's nearly as big as the museum itself. This traditional fieldstone farmhouse is tiny by modern standards, with a single room on each of its two floors, but it makes a cosy museum. It is small enough that there's no risk of being overwhelmed by the number of displays, yet important enough that you'll see excellent exhibitions, carefully researched and elegantly presented. Depending on the current theme, you might get the chance to take a close-up look at costumes from famous theatrical productions or simply find out what's hip today. And there's always something for children to do on a Sunday afternoon.

The house, built in 1750, was one of the first in St Lambert. Its construction is typical of the period, with bell-cast eves extending over a front porch and dormers projecting from the roof. (Dormers were popular at the time—they turned a second floor into living space, although it was only taxed as an attic.)

The house has been renovated many times over the years, but its wide-plank wooden floors and exposed beams are original. And though the museum is a mere stone's throw from Highway 20, it has a warm, homey feeling you'd expect in a place tucked away in the countryside. Despite its smallness, earlier in this century four families lived there!

98 Get Outta Town!

The Marsil Museum points out that clothing, as a universal part of the human experience, reflects not just personal taste, but political, economic, and cultural values as well. In "Common Threads: Cloth, Clothing, and Culture," for example, one display showed how much a timeless Inuit *amauti* and a 1950s Christian Dior original have in common. Another illustrated the similarities between Ghandi's homespun cloth and the Quebec *étoffe du pays*, a hooded coat of grey homespun wool worn by *patriotes* of the rebellion of 1837.

Very rare and remarkable clothing and fabric are often on display. One exhibition featured a Victorian ball gown decorated with hundreds of pearls. But the museum is very much grounded in the community. During the "Cool Clothes" exhibition, grade-school students were asked to lend their favourite article of clothing and to tell the story behind it.

This is a small museum with a long reach. Most of the exhibitions are organized in conjunction with other institutions, which have included the Museum for Textiles (Toronto), the McCord Museum of Canadian History (Montreal), and the Canadian Museum of Civilization (Hull). The results are always enjoyable. Repeat visitors will note how remarkably the layout can change from one exhibition to the next.

The museum's reputation for excellence means that it can often catch travelling exhibitions as they make their way around the continent. In 1995, for example, the museum featured an exhibition of quilts, showcasing 20 of the country's top works, both traditional and modern. It was the first time the triennial event, sponsored by Rodman Hall (of St Catherines, Ontario) had found its way to a museum in Quebec.

The museum is set up for school groups, so there is always a hands-on activity for those who get fidgety. Children of all ages will enjoy the Sunday workshops (2 p.m.–4 p.m.). Keep an eye out for the special Christmas workshops held in early December.

SEASON AND HOURS
10 a.m.–4 p.m., Tues–Fri; 1 p.m.–4 p.m, Sat–Sun; all year.
Closed between exhibitions.

FEES
Adults $2, students and seniors $1, children under 12 free.

INFORMATION
671-3098.

DIRECTIONS
Take the Champlain Bridge (staying in the right-hand lane) and follow Highway 20 east towards Longueuil to exit 6. The museum is on the corner of Riverside and Notre Dame.

Montérégie

Montérégie is a huge tourist region. Starting due west of Montreal, it wraps southward around the

Photo: Centre de la Conservation de la Nature Mont St Hilaire

city, then turns north with the Richelieu River, extending as far east as the Eastern Townships and Coeur du Québec. It is a mainly agricultural area, with well-preserved woodlands, some mountains, and a wealth of waterways unmatched in the rest of the province.

Montrealers often zip through on the way to Vermont or New York, but this is a shame. For the daytripper, Montérégie offers activities all year long: apple picking in the fall; cross-country skiing, skating, and snow shoeing in the winter.  The region is rich in history and has two forts on the Richelieu River and one on the St Lawrence. If that's not enough, Montérégie also has a number of excellent sandy beaches.

 Museums, a bee farm, a reptile vivarium, a science centre, and a bird sanctuary are described here, plus a surprise from Ontario: Cooper Marsh, just across the border, is a beautiful spot, and well worth a visit.

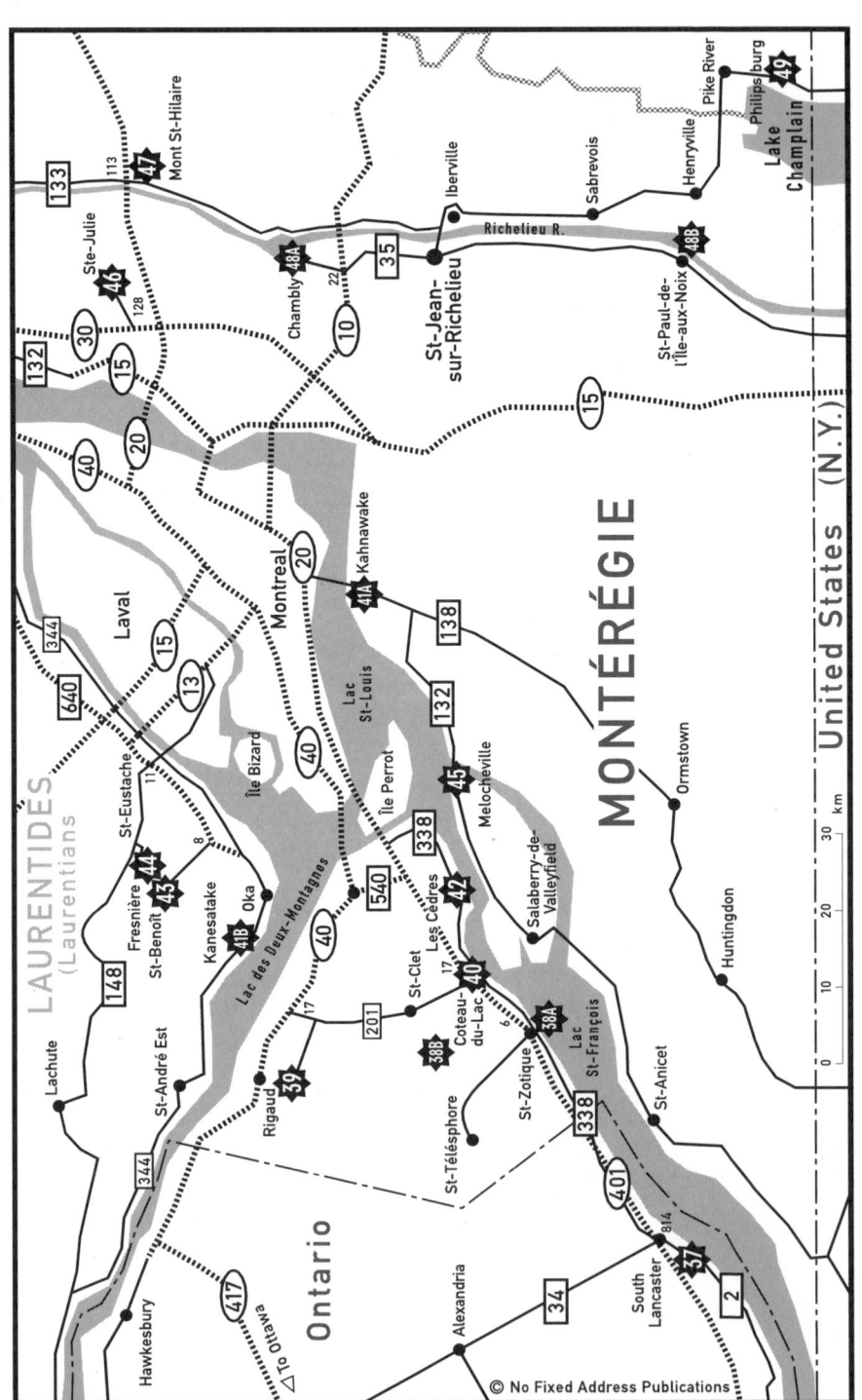

MONTÉRÉGIE

Trip Destinations

37 Cooper Marsh Conservation Area
South Lancaster, Ont.
(613) 347-1332
p.104

38A St Zotique Municipal Beach
St Zotique
(514) 267-9335
p.106

38B Le Sablon Beach, St Polycarpe
(514) 265-3564, (800) 267-3564
p.106

39 Sucrerie de la Montagne, Rigaud
(514) 451-5204
p.108

40 Coteau du Lac National Historic Site, Coteau du Lac
(514) 763-5631
p.110

41A Kanesatake Powwow, Kanesatake
(514) 479-8811, (514) 479-8093
p.112

41B Kahnawake Powwow, Kahnawake
(514) 632-8667
p.112

42 Centre Plein Air Les Forestiers
Les Cèdres
(514) 452-4736
p.114

43 Hydromelerie Intermiel
(Bee Farm), St Benoît

(514) 258-2713
or (800) 265-MIEL (6435)
p.116

44 Exotarium (Reptile Vivarium)
Fresnière (near St. Eustache)
(514) 472-1827
p.118

45 Pointe du Buisson Archaeological Dig, Melocheville
(514) 429-7857
p.120

46 Électrium, St Julie
(514) 652-8977
p.122

47 Centre de Conservation de la Nature Mont St Hilaire,
Mont St Hilaire
(514) 467-1755
p.124

48A Fort Chambly National Historic Site, St Jean sur Richelieu
(514) 658-1585
p.126

48B Fort Lennox National Historic Site
St Paul de Île aux Noix
(514) 658-1585
p.126

49 George H. Montgomery Bird Sanctuary, Philipsburg
(514) 637-2141
p.128

Tourist Information

Montérégie Tourist Association
(514) 674-5555

Chambly Tourist Bureau (seasonal)
(514) 658-0321

Mont St Hilaire (seasonal)
(514) 446-1833

Salaberry de Valleyfield Tourist Bureau
(514) 377-3727

St Jean sur Richelieu Tourist Bureau
(514) 346-4943

St Paul de l'Île aux Noix (seasonal)
(514) 246-3227

Cooper Marsh
Conservation Area
South Lancaster, Ont.
DRIVING TIME: 1 HR 15 MIN

Birders know the best bird-watching is at dawn and dusk, but at Cooper Marsh, late risers finally get a break. Things are happening all day long in this conservation area on the St Lawrence's Lake St Francis, just across the Ontario border. In addition to dozens of species of waterfowl and songbirds, you might see a muskrat scampering along a boardwalk, a raccoon in a tree, or snapping turtles and frogs in the water. A fine interpretation centre with a friendly staff adds to the pleasure, but the great fun is in walking across wetlands without getting your feet wet!

The marsh features a series of easy walks through various habitats. Wherever you go, you'll hear quacking, chirping, and a great harmonious mix of birdsong, the buzz of insects, and the trickling of water. Oddly enough, there are no mosquitoes or swamp gas to contend with.

Trails are clearly marked with animal- and colour-coded signs. The Muskrat Motor (3 km) is the longest walk, along the top of the marsh's main dyke. It is also the most rugged, but has benches for resting and is a good place for fans of muskrats, mink, and snapping turtles. The Heron Hike (2 km) follows another dyke.

The Swallow Swirl (1 km) and Mallard March (1.3 km) are excellent.

MONTÉRÉGIE

Both have long stretches of wide and sturdy boardwalks with solid railings. The Swallow Swirl is a very romantic trail leading through treed marsh (a swamp, by definition). The Mallard March winds across emergent vegetation, cattails, and open water (a marsh). It also has a tower and duck blinds for observing the wildlife.

Panels (in French and English) explain the local ecosystems. For example, in addition to supporting an incredible diversity of wildlife, marshlands are nature's kidneys, breaking down complex chemicals (including phosphates) and purifying the water table. The oily film you might see is not pollution; rather, it's a sign the wetland is doing its job.

Construction of the St Lawrence Seaway in 1959 resulted in fluctuating water levels in the marsh, and completion of a generating station at Cornwall lowered it permanently. When cottages and development further threatened the area in the '70s, Bill Cooper rallied groups to begin purchasing the land. Ducks Unlimited lent their expertise to build the first dykes, and Cooper Marsh was born.

The best environment for waterfowl is half open water and half vegetation, but that balance couldn't exist at this marsh without help. Every spring, water is pumped into the marsh, and it filters out naturally as the season progresses. While the water is still too crowded with vegetation, the marsh is by all counts a success, the number of bird species jumped from 12 to the current 150, though they're not all in one tree!

The modern visitor's centre fits right into its surroundings. Exhibits include mounted birds and decoys, plus some live creatures, such as a praying mantis and a snapping turtle. Seasonal events include lectures, workshops, and bird-banding expeditions. There is no snack bar, but there is a nice picnic area at the entrance, with a barbecue pit and tables in the shade of half a dozen large weeping willows.

SEASON AND HOURS
Visitor's centre: 8:30 a.m.–4:30 p.m., every day, all year; conservation area open 24 hr. Guided tours at 2:00 p.m. on weekends.

FEES
Free.

INFORMATION
(613) 347-1332.

DIRECTIONS
Take Highway 20 or Highway 40 (Trans-Canada) west towards Toronto. In Ontario, Highway 20 becomes Highway 401. Take exit 814 (Lancaster–Alexandria) and turn south on Highway 2. Follow for 3 km, through South Lancaster to the marsh entrance, on the south side of the highway.

Two Sandy Beaches
of Montérégie
West of Montreal
DRIVING TIME: 40-50 MIN

You're bound to feel right at home on the small beach run by the Municipality of St Zotique. Most visitors to this nice stretch of yellow sand are families and groups of teenagers from the city. Hosts in blue shirts with "Welcome" written in English, French, Spanish, Italian, and German will make sure you're getting the most out of your day in the sun.

This very pleasant beach has 125 m of supervised swimming, and water that deepens (as at most beaches on the St Lawrence's lakes) very slowly to 1.70 m. You can rent sailboards and sailboats (special ones for 8- to 12-year-olds) or you can explore the canals of the nearby cottage community in a pedal boat. Interestingly, the canal walls are of cedar, since concrete has been forbidden on the St Lawrence for some time.

Wine and beer (in plastic bottles and cans only) are permitted on the beach, or you can settle in at one of the 650 picnic tables in one of the large shaded grassy areas. You can even bring your own barbecue or purchase snacks at the lunch counter.

The mini golf course (fee applies), the great little playground, and especially the supervised wading pool, will delight kids. The wading pool has giant mushroom-shaped fountains, a variety of sprinklers, and pint-sized slides. There are a couple of nice tennis courts (free, but bring your own rackets), and you can play volleyball on dry courts or one in the water (deposit required for balls).

To really get in over your head—in terms of both water and beach culture—go inland to St Polycarpe. As teenagers we used to sneak into this abandoned sandpit, where the water was up to 14 m deep. Now, umpteen years later, **Le Sablon** is a privately run beach. Don't be fooled by the somewhat lunar entrance: the beach area is beautifully landscaped and fringed by tall white pines. Dozens of activities and services, and a youthful crowd, make this the Baywatch of Quebec and the beach of choice for a fun-packed day.

The main beach is a wide crescent of white sand sloping down to a deep, spring-fed sandy lake of a remarkable blue tint. A DJ plays alternative pop tunes at a reasonable volume over-crisp sounding speakers, and there's a beach house with a canteen, convenience store, bar, dance floor, changing rooms, and free security lockers.

Half a dozen beach volleyball courts are available for pickup games or organized tournaments. You might want to get into shape for the annual bathing beauty contest: there's even a men's division, Monsieur Beau-Bonhomme. The gang also organizes dances on the beach and tugs of war in water. The inner-tube slide is a hoot, and in a deeper area, you can go ape on the supervised Tarzan-type swing before dropping 4 m into the water.

You can rent pedal boats, canoes, aquabikes, and sailboards, or go galloping through the dunes on horseback, rent mountain bikes, or try your hand at archery. For those who want to make a weekend of it, Le Sablon also has a 90-site campground.

SEASON AND HOURS
Both beaches: 9 a.m.–8 p.m., every day, mid-June–end of August.

FEES
St Zotique: Adults $6, under 12 free.
Le Sablon: Adults $7, students $6, children 6–11 $4, under 6 free.

INFORMATION
St Zotique Beach (514) 267-9335;
Le Sablon (514) 265-3564 or (800) 267-3564.

DIRECTIONS
Take Highway 20 (Trans-Canada) west to exit 6 (St Zotique). For St Zotique, turn south and follow signs to the beach, just west of town. For Le Sablon, head north 5 km in the direction of St Télésphore. Follow the blue panel signs to the entrance, on Chemin St Philippe.

Sucrerie de la Montagne
Rigaud
DRIVING TIME: 50 MIN

When Sandy and Pierre Faucher opened up their sugar bush on the edge of Rigaud Mountain 20 years ago, they had something special in mind. They wanted to create a place where visitors could spend the better part of the day learning how maple syrup is made, hiking or skiing the trails, and dining on fine traditional sugarhouse food—all the while basking in the ambience of pioneer life in Quebec. The operation is now one of the biggest in the region, but it still retains a very cosy feeling. Sugaring off is from March to May, but at the Sucrerie you'll find fun and entertainment year round.

The Sucrerie is modelled after a traditional sugar bush and logging camp. Buildings include a working sawmill at the entrance, a general store, where you can pick up maple treats and gifts, and the sugarhouse, where the sap is boiled for hours on end to reduce it to maple syrup. In all, about half a dozen log and fieldstone cabins are set in a large grove of tall maple trees, cleared of undergrowth.

One of the Fauchers, clad in pioneer clothing, greets each group of guests

108 Get Outta Town!

and leads a tour of the facilities. In the sugarhouse, you'll learn how trees are tapped and how wood-fired evaporators work. There are no vacuum tubes and pumps here—sap is collected the traditional way, using a horse and sleigh to do the rounds, and emptying the buckets one by one. On a windless day, the plinking of droplets falling into over 5,000 buckets sounds like music.

Every building has a bit of history in it, and objects of interest are tucked into every corner. Children will love the main lodge with its bearskin rugs and old photographs on the walls, stuffed and mounted birds in the rafters, and Coco the parrot, very much alive, squawking on his perch.

Many rooms have a fireplace or antique stove. The giant fieldstone oven in the bakery, for example, can bake 120 loaves of bread at one time—provided someone gets up at 5 a.m. to stoke the fire. The fireplace in the main lodge dining room, however, takes the prize. It is a fabulous fieldstone and brick affair, straight out of *Citizen Kane*, with a hearth 6 m long and 1.5 m high.

The dining room is large but cosy, with hand-hewn beams and wooden floors. Each beautifully laid pine banquet table has an oil lamp on it. The menu is traditional, and includes pea soup, fresh bread, baked beans, relishes, and plenty of maple syrup, of course. Everything is made on the premises, including a sumptuous maple-glazed smoked ham.

The wine list includes red or white wine, blueberry wine, and the traditional drink of Quebec woodsmen, caribou—the white lightning of Quebec. According to the Fauchers, you can drink up to eight glasses of caribou before you start growing horns. Live music will keep you entertained during your meal, and young ones will be invited to learn to tap spoons, sing, and dance.

If you want to spend the night, you can rest up in one of four log cabins, then hike, snowshoe, or cross-country ski on 40 km of trails.

SEASON AND HOURS
All year. Sugaring off is in spring, generally mid-Mar–mid-Apr.

FEES
Tour: Free. Table d'hôte dining: approximately $30 per adult.

INFORMATION
(514) 451-5204.

DIRECTIONS
Take Highway 20 or 40 (Trans-Canada) west, then branch north onto Highway 417 to Ottawa, to exit 17 (Montée Lavigne–St Clet). Turn left onto Route 201 south. After 2–3 km, turn right onto Rang St Georges, a beautiful road winding up the side of Mount Rigaud. The Sucrerie is at 300 Rang St Georges, 6 km along, on the right-hand side. (It is clearly signposted from Highway 417.)

Coteau du Lac
National Historic Site
Coteau du Lac

DRIVING TIME: 45 MIN

Photo: J. Beardsell / Parks Canada

In 1780, the first gated canal in North America was built, at Coteau du Lac. It was 100 m long by 1.8 m wide, and held only 80 cm of water—not exactly big enough for today's lakers, but it got the flat-bottomed Durham boats past the fiercest rapids on the St Lawrence. Subsequent canals and dams have since robbed the rapids of their former glory, but they are still very pretty. At Coteau du Lac, you can tour the ruins of fortifications, stroll the dry canal bed, and enjoy a lovely view of the St Lawrence and Delisle rivers.

A path leads from the parking lot to a modern visitor's centre, and from there through the grounds. It goes past various ruins, cannons facing the river, and the rapids themselves, with well-written panels describing each area. Large metal sculptures throughout the site evoke images from the past, and guides in period costume are on hand to answer questions. There are also some great ramparts, perfect for rolling down—but keep an eye out for groundhog holes!

An octagonal blockhouse has been rebuilt where it protected the canal during the War of 1812, when up to 3,000 soldiers were stationed here. It houses some historical items, and offers bird's-eye views of the river.

The lock, now high and dry, is decorated with the silhouettes of workers digging, and contains a sculpture of one of the Durham boats that navigated it. This flat-bottomed boat with pointed ends looks like an English punting boat. Though the original precanal portage was only 60 paces, these boats had to be unloaded, hauled through the rapids, and reloaded downstream.

The lock, British built, is actually predated by a canal built by the French in 1759. It was a narrow channel on the river's edge, protected from the rapids by a dike made of stone, wood, and earth. (It doesn't qualify as a lock, though, since it lacked gates.) You'll need a good eye to spot the ruins of the first canal on the exposed granite of the river. It may not look like much now, but keep in mind that the river was almost 3 m higher in those days, and these were the most turbulent rapids on the St Lawrence, dropping 2 m locally, and 25 m over 12 km.

Canals, like roads, require rebuilding, and in 1845 the Coteau du Lac Canal was superseded by the first Beauharnois Canal, dug on the south side of the St Lawrence. That, in turn, was replaced by the Soulange Canal, built in 1899 on the north side. The St Lawrence Seaway is the most recent project. It was completed in 1959, on the site of the original Beauharnois Canal.

Unfortunately, picnicking is not permitted on the lovely grounds, though there are a number of shaded benches where a quick snack might be taken. Luckily, there is a park nearby, just west along Chemin du Fleuve (River Rd), with a huge 16-m maple tree that provides ample shade on a sunny day. You'll recognize the park by the baseball diamond, visible from the road.

If you'd prefer to dine, try the nearby Maison du Tourisme. Its patio extends over the Delisle River, which generates most of the restaurant's power. Inside, try to spy the faces in the rocks—you'll see a smiling old grandfather and a young woman on the walls.

SEASON AND HOURS
10:00 a.m.–6:00 p.m., every day, mid-May–mid-Oct.

FEES
Site: Free.
Visitor's centre and blockhouse: Adults $2.50, children 6–16 $1.25, family $5.25.

INFORMATION
(514) 763-5631.

DIRECTIONS
Take Highway 20 west to exit 17 (Coteau du Lac). Follow the signs from there. For a more scenic drive, take Route 338 south from Dorion and along the Soulange Canal. In summer, the canal is active with kayakers, scuba divers, picnickers, and people fishing.

Indian Powwows
Kahnawake
and Kanesatake

DRIVING TIME: 20 MIN & 50 MIN

Each year, on the weekend closest to July 11 (the anniversary of the Oka crisis), Montreal's Mohawk communities invite Natives and non-Natives alike to their powwows, traditional festivities of dance and music. For some of the finest dancing on the continent, visit the competitive powwow at Kahnawake. For a less crowded and more laid-back experience, drop by Kanesatake. Whichever you choose, you'll enjoy the friendly crowds, tasty food, and excellent dancing, drumming, and singing.

Of the 500 or so Indian powwows in North America, the one on Tekakwitha Island in **Kahnawake** is the fastest growing. The stands are packed and there is standing room only when competitors from across the continent vie for over $30,000 in prize money.

Over the two days of the powwow, you'll see fancy dances, jingle dances, grass dances, and other traditional dances. Some of the men look truly fierce in their feathers and black makeup as they perform the sneak-up, commemorating the hunt. In the fancy dance, performers must know the steps and music intimately, timing the last step of their fast-paced dance with the last beat of the drum. Grass dancing enacts the stomping out of prairie grass fires. Each tribe has its own specialty, though some dances are shared by many tribes.

The costumes are marvellous. The women's are generally of a softer cut than the men's and are often decorated with up to 10 kg of beadwork and bells.

MONTÉRÉGIE

Starting Saturday at 9 a.m., you can take in the large arts and crafts sale or sample exotic foods such as buffalo burgers and Micmac salmon at over 50 food stalls. The Grand Entry at noon marks the beginning of the powwow. It is an impressive ceremony, led by elders carrying honour staffs decorated with medicines and feathers. The retiring of the flags closes the day at 7 p.m.

The **Kanesatake** powwow, held the same weekend, is more traditional. It has a very spiritual feel to it, with Indians coming from across Canada, the U.S., and as far away as Ecuador to dance for their Creator. You'll see a variety of excellent performances and have the chance to join in the fun during the intertribal dances. How often do you get to dance beside a fully costumed Mohawk warrior?

The chanting and drumming emanates from a central arbour, where musicians sit under the protective medicine of cedar branches. A master of ceremonies explains the significance of each dance. On the Friday before the weekend, a parade leads from the town of Oka, past the infamous pines, to the powwow grounds. Some years, early birds can join the tobacco burning and prayer ceremony at sunrise.

There are some stands, but you might want to bring a blanket or lawn chairs and a picnic hamper. There are fewer food and crafts stalls at Kanesatake, but you'll still get a chance to sample Native fare, including a delicious corn soup. If you'd like to spend the weekend, you can bring a tent. Even if you don't stay over, take a stroll through the camping area for a great view from the little beach on the tip of the peninsula. (Swimming is not allowed.)

Kahnawake
SEASON AND HOURS
9 a.m.–7 p.m. (dancing from 1 p.m.), Sat–Sun, weekend nearest July 11.
FEES
General $8, youth 13–17 $4, elders and children 6-12 $3, children under 6 free.
INFORMATION
(514) 632-8667.
DIRECTIONS
Take the Mercier Bridge heading towards Route 138. Follow the signs for Kahnawake.

Kanesatake
SEASON AND HOURS
10 a.m.–late, Sat–Sun, weekend nearest July 11.
FEES
General $6, elders and children under 12 free.
INFORMATION
(514) 479-8811 or (514) 479-8093.
DIRECTIONS
Take Highway 15 (Laurentian Autoroute) north to Highway 640. Follow the 640 west to the end, and continue on Route 344 through Oka to Kanesatake.

Winter Activities
at the Centre Plein Air
Les Forestiers
Les Cèdres
DRIVING TIME: 40 MIN

Photo: Centre Plein Air Les Forestiers

J ust off the western tip of the Island of Montreal, the Centre Plein Air Les Forestiers is a real gem. In an area not particularly well known as a cold-season getaway, the friendly staff of this non-profit organization serve up a real smorgasbord of winter activities. The centre offers some great novice cross-country ski trails, a nicely maintained skating ring not too far from shelter, and a really zippy little tobogganing slope. A canine club makes the centre just a little bit livelier, and you'll more than likely get to see a dogsled team or two running along the trails.

All activities start from the visitor's centre, which is a basic ski lodge with a short-order kitchen and a large eating area. On weekends, there is a wood-burning stove to keep you toasty warm and a daycare centre for children too young to join the outdoor fun.

Les Forestiers is a great place to get a taste for cross-country skiing. You can rent a variety of equipment, including baby gliders—the toboggans you tow behind you. The centre boasts a 35-km network of patrolled trails across mainly flat terrain. Most trails lead through the woods, so are protected from

114 Get Outta Town!

the wind, and all are beautifully maintained. In fact, this is one of the rare centres that owns a Bombardier BR160 grooming machine, which it uses after each snowfall. This expensive machine can carve two trails simultaneously, bank curves, and adjust its pitch and pressure to snow conditions. It can also groom a flat portion for skate-skiing, but if you like a backwoods experience, take heart—7 km are left ungroomed, just for you.

Other winter activities include kicksledding, skating, and tobogganing. Kicksleds resemble small dogsleds, but they are human powered. One person sits, while the other pushes from behind, jumping on for the downhill runs. This new sport is really catching on—especially with those on the sitting end of the deal! Just outside the visitor's centre door there is a 400-m circular skating track, and nearby is a terrific toboggan run, down a sandpit "bowl." You can bring your own toboggan, or rent a giant fabric-covered inner tube for a wild ride down this rather steep pitch. A staircase, faithfully cleared of snow, makes the climb back up much easier.

If you have a hardy dog, you might be interested in the canine club that operates out of the centre. There are 12 km of separate trails for dogs and their owners, specifically for dogsledding and "ski joring."

Ski joring originated in Scandinavia, where it involved skiers pulled by horses. Here, the sport has been combined with the Canadian tradition of dogsledding, and ski jorers are pulled by (or ski with) their own dogs, attached by a special harness. According to the experts, most dogs will enjoy the sport, though they usually require some special training, since untrained dogs can get out of control with sled dogs around. (Equipment is available. Call the centre for details.)

SEASON AND HOURS
Winter: 8:30 a.m.–4:30 p.m., Mon–Fri; 8:30 a.m.–5:30 p.m., Sat–Sun.
Summer: 8:30 a.m.–4:30 p.m., Mon–Fri; weekends by reservation.

FEES
Adults $7, youth 7–19 $5, under 6 free, family $20. Rental: Inner-tube $2 per hour, $5 per day; kicksled $6 per hour; skis and snowshoes available.

INFORMATION
Centre (514) 452-4736.

DIRECTIONS
Take Highway 20 or Highway 40 (Trans-Canada) west to exit 22 (Chemin St Dominique), just past Les Cèdres. Follow Chemin St Dominique north, across Route 340, along several kilometres, and up a small hill. Just past a heavy-machinery school, the road forks. Go right. The centre is a couple of kilometres along, on the left.

Hydromelerie Intermiel
Bee Farm
St Benoît, near Oka
DRIVING TIME: 1 HR

D irectly between Oka and St Eustache, as the bee flies, is the Hydromelerie Intermiel, where the ancient art of beekeeping is alive and well. *Hydromel* is French for mead, the delicious alcoholic beverage that predates even wine and beer, and *miel* means honey. For Vivian and Christian Macle, tending 1,600 hives that produce some 90 t of honey per season is a full-time occupation. They offer day-trippers a splendid opportunity to spend a couple of hours visiting the operation, learning about bees, browsing in the boutique, and sampling their many honey-based products.

Tours in French or English cover all bases, from extracting the honey through bee viewing to mead making (and tasting!). Honey extraction is a simple yet delicate process in which the honeycomb is warmed, then spun in a centrifuge resembling a giant lettuce dryer. Finally, the wax plugs are separated from the honey itself. Of course, no understanding of the process would be complete without tasting the 11 kinds of honey produced at Intermiel, including chocolate honey.

One bee-viewing area is the screened-off balcony beside three hives. Beekeeper René Desprès, smoker in hand, opens up a hive or two to show you the queen, workers, drones, and combs. Each hive can contain up to

MONTÉRÉGIE

12,000 busy bees and produces about 30 kg of honey every two weeks. The only danger in working with bees, René claims, is that you could end up with an ear full of honey!

Just off the balcony is the discovery room, where six hives share a large floor-to-ceiling bee condominium. You can get as close as you like to the 70,000–80,000 inhabitants, separated from you and neighbouring hives by thick glass. A tunnel leads outdoors from each hive. You can watch the bees scurrying about, depositing honey in the combs. For a real thrill, put your ear to the glass.

Intermiel makes 30,000–35,000 bottles of mead each year, in a very high-tech set-up. Mead (called "honey wine" under Quebec law) is made of yeast and two parts water to one part honey. The mixture is put into giant stainless-steel containers, and 10 weeks late, presto—the mead is ready.

You can sample seven kinds of mead at Intermiel, ranging from dry with a hint of honey to very sweet and highly alcoholic. The raspberry mead gets my vote for its lightly honeyed taste with a raspberry tang.

Between samples, there are interesting beekeeping facts to be learned. For example, it is completely normal for honey to crystallize, and you should be wary of honey that supposedly does not. To return honey to its liquid form, just sit the jar in warm water—don't microwave it. Also, there are different theories about why smoke pacifies bees. One thing known for sure is that smoke causes bees to eat their honey. So either they can't curl their honey-filled abdomens enough to sting, or they're too happy to want to.

The Hydromelerie has a lovely country boutique with over 60 products. Not all are made in-house, but all are produced with their own honey. They sell beeswax candles, mustards, relishes, royal jelly, propolis, and pollen. The pollen-and-honey shampoo and a full line of cosmetics, most containing honey and propolis, are very popular. And so, of course, is the mead, at $8–$12 per bottle.

SEASON AND HOURS
9 a.m.–6 p.m., every day, all year. Bee viewing on the screened porch in warmer months only.

FEES
Free.

INFORMATION
(514) 258-2713 or
(800) 265-MIEL (6435).

DIRECTIONS
Take Highway 640 west (towards Oka) to exit 8. Follow the signs to Hydromelerie Intermiel, about 20 km from the exit. Intermiel is located at 10291 La Fresnière. A nice way to return to the city is via the Oka–Hudson ferry.

Exotarium
Reptile Vivarium
Fresnière
(near St Eustache)
DRIVING TIME: 1 HR

If you like creepy-crawlies and things that go squish in the night, you'll love the Exotarium. At a safe distance from Montreal, it is one of only two or three reptile breeding centres in Canada that opens its doors—though not its cage doors!—to the general public. It is a fascinating and educational place, absolutely bursting with snakes, alligators, crocodiles, water monitors, gila monsters, frogs, turtles—just about every reptile under the sun, and some spiders and cockroaches for added interest.

Co-owner and chief handler Hervé Maranda's passion for reptiles began when he was four, chasing lizards while on holiday in the south of France. Not satisfied with collecting just the tails, he began breeding reptiles for pet shops and zoos in 1986. He was soon joined by Martina Schneider, another enthusiast. They married and opened the Exotarium in 1990.

Highlights include two African dwarf crocodiles that are very much like concrete lawn ornaments—until they bark. There are a couple of enormous Burmese pythons coiled together in a large enclosure, plus a num-

MONTÉRÉGIE

ber of poisonous snakes, including a Palestinian viper, a spitting cobra, and a rattlesnake that really rattles! All reptiles, poisonous or not, are safely behind glass.

Some of the reptiles are truly beautiful. The White's tree frog (native to Australia and New Guinea) has the colour and sheen of aquamarine porcelain. The two tomato frogs would indeed look at home in a bowl of salad. But the South African horned frog is, in my opinion, the fairest of them all. Richly decorated in a mosaic of bright colours, it looks very much like an ornate Japanese teacup.

Some are just plain bizarre looking. Prime examples are the pig-nosed turtle with a snout adapted for sniffing out food and a spiny turtle with a snake-like neck as long as its body. This place has everything, including a pit with three alligators, a crocodile, turtles, and a catwalk from which to observe them.

Mr. Maranda's show-and-tell is great, but not for the faint of heart. Things start off rather calmly with a blue-tongued skink. Looking like a cross between a snake and an uncooked breakfast sausage, this friendly lizard with stumpy legs likes getting to know you with a very active blue tongue. Next, things get a little hairier with a tarantula the size of a saucer. You can pet him, and even let him crawl across your hand. The grand finale is the 3-m boa constrictor. Believe it or not, even the four- and five-year-olds were delighted to have this sleepy creature draped around their necks!

Boas, by the way, have very poor eyesight and are almost deaf. They make up for it with incredible heat-sensing organs believed to allow them to form a 3D image of their prey. Sensitive to variations in temperature of as little as one hundredth of a degree Celsius, they can even differentiate between a vein and an artery. But don't worry; contrary to popular opinion, reptiles cannot smell fear!

SEASON AND HOURS
12 p.m.–5 p.m.; Fri–Sun and holiday Mondays, Sept–June (closed Jan); every day (except Wed), July–Aug.

FEES
Adults $5, children 3–16 $3.50, family $16. Special group rates.

INFORMATION
(514) 472-1827.

DIRECTIONS
Take Highway 15 (Laurentian Autoroute) north to Highway 640. Follow the 640 west to exit 11 (Lachute). Go west along Arthur Sauvé Blvd (Route 148) 200 m, and turn left just past the hospital onto Industrial Blvd. At Fresnière, turn right, and continue north to the Exotarium. (Total distance from exit 11 is 7 km.)

Get Outta Town! 119

Pointe du Buisson
Archaeological Dig
Melocheville

DRIVING TIME: 30 MIN

Photo: Pointe du Buisson Archaeological Park

For 5,000 years before the arrival of Europeans, Pointe du Buisson (Scrub Point), a wooded peninsula jutting out into rapids on the St Lawrence just southwest of Montreal, was a summer campground for Native Canadians. The point was a natural resting place during the portage around the rapids, but it was the bounty of sturgeon that kept them coming back, summer after summer. The last tribes abandoned the area in the 15th century, leaving behind a wealth of information about themselves. Pointe du Buisson is now a working archaeological site with a visitor's centre and museum, plus wooded walks and a wonderful view of the St Lawrence.

The visitor's centre is a modern, ecologically designed building at the entrance. Since it also serves as the research centre, there isn't much on display here, though a model of the site and an ancient dugout canoe can provide some distraction for little ones while big ones sort through pamphlets and maps. A dozen tables on a wooden deck shaded by the forest are nice for a picnic, and food can be purchased in the snack bar.

On the tip of the peninsula, a short walk from the visitor's centre, is the museum, a small unpainted wooden structure built into a hillside. It presents the story of the people who lived here from 3000 BC to AD 1400. It has great dioramas of fishing practices, showing both the activity above the water and the fish below. The Indians fished for sturgeon using hemp gillnets, by torch at night, or using a mesh wall and spears. And these were no little panfish. The largest sturgeon caught this century, for example, was 2.41 m long, and weighed in at 140 kg!

The Indians preserved their catch by smoking it, and on weekends in summer your admission ticket includes a taste of smoked sturgeon, store-bought, but heated over an open fire. (The construction of the Beauharnois hydro-electric dam brought an end to the fishing.)

Other exhibits include a terrific display of the awls, cutting edges, and other implements used by Indians in daily activities, with an explanation of how the tools were made (pick up the English version by the door). Stone cutting edges were made using a technique called pressure-flaking. After the shape was roughly fashioned, an antler was used to apply great pressure to the edge. This delicate and time-consuming operation caused tiny chips to pop off the rock, resulting in an edge as sharp as that of a steel knife.

The archaeological excavation takes place on the wide lawn between the museum and the river. But you won't see any long dusty trenches or bucket bearers here. The wells are less than a metre square, and the bedrock is a mere 15–30 cm beneath the soil. Five thousand years of history in so little soil means the peninsula is extremely rich in artifacts—so far, over a million have been unearthed.

Two or three paths meander through the forest. The nicest one is the Chemin du Portage, with two wooden footbridges crossing over deep ravines. Be sure to bring insect repellent before venturing into the woods in summer!

There are two special weekends each summer, usually in late July and early August. On Indian Heritage Day you can feast on smoked sturgeon and roast corn, watch traditional dancing, listen to stories, light a fire using a flint, or make a mask. On Archaeological Day you get to help out in the dig—and you're guaranteed to find an artifact.

The museum and grounds are wheelchair accessible.

SEASON AND HOURS
10 a.m.–5 p.m., Mon–Fri,
10 a.m.–6 p.m., Sat–Sun, mid-May–Labour Day. 12 p.m.–5 p.m., Sat–Sun, Labour Day–Thanksgiving.
ADMISSION
Adults $4, seniors $3, children $2.
INFORMATION
(514) 429-7857.
DIRECTIONS
Take the Mercier Bridge, and follow Route 132 west.

Électrium
St Julie

DRIVING TIME: 25 MIN

Just off Highway 30 near Mount St Bruno is Hydro-Québec's research centre, an imposing building framed by giant electrical towers. Nearby, and considerably smaller, is the Électrium, the utility's Electricity and Magnetic Field Interpretation Centre. That's a rather formal name for a place that is anything but daunting. The Électrium has a friendly staff and excellent facilities. Thanks to its Van de Graaff generator, you no longer have to visit Ottawa's Science Centre for a hair-raising adventure in the world of science.

There are plenty of buttons to push and wheels to crank during the fun but informative tour offered by the bilingual staff. The 1.5 hr tour examines a host of topics, from electricity in nature (including the human body) to the physics of electricity, and the nature of electrical and magnetic fields. It's a chance to learn the difference between direct current, alternating current, and static electricity. All demonstrations are picture-perfect and clearly explained. (Recommended for ages 10 and up.)

One display presents animals that can perceive magnetic fields or electric potential (voltage), like homing pigeons, sea turtles, and sharks. The *pièce de résistance* is the large aquarium housing an electric eel. Native to Brazil, electric eels are blind, and produce electric jolts to sound out their surroundings, in much the same way as bats use radar. The eels can also give off shocks of up to 650 V. That's enough to stun, kill, or maybe even reheat the eel's dinner (usually a small frog) from up to a metre away.

MONTÉRÉGIE

Other highlights of the tour include an oscilloscope for measuring your heartbeat, a battery made out of a grapefruit, and game to test your reaction time to light and sound. There are more sophisticated demonstrations, as well. For example, a heavy wire surrounded by dozens of compasses illustrates the well-known principle that a flow of electricity creates a magnetic field. Pressing a button causes a current to run through the wire. The needles of the compasses, initially pointing north, swing to follow the new magnetic field.

A fascinating and well-made 8-min film explains the electrical phenomena of lightning and the northern lights. In short, lightning occurs when raindrops blown upwards brush against hailstones falling downwards in the same cloud, exchanging charges. The flash is the re-establishment of equilibrium. It heats the surrounding air to 30,000°C, carries a charge of several hundred million volts, and is as bright as a 50,000-W light bulb. But, if you were to harness that energy, it would power a 60-W light bulb for only 10 days. The northern lights are caused when solar particles enter the atmosphere at the poles, where the earth's magnetic field is weakest.

Around the final corner is a full-sized kitchen. With the help of a hand-held meter, you can measure the magnetic fields of common appliances. A microwave oven radiates a field of 100 microteslas (μT) at the motor, but at the door the reading is 20 μT. A stove element produces 160 μT up close, but the reading is lower farther away. Outside, the high-tension wires produces 20 μT, measured from the ground. In comparison, the earth has a magnetic field of 50 μT. (Unlike the other fields, however, the earth's does not alternate, so it doesn't induce a current.) Nevertheless, Hydro-Québec and the Électrium maintain there are no studies proving that magnetic fields affect living organisms.

SEASON AND HOURS
June–Aug: 9:30 a.m.–4:00 p.m., every day.
Sept–May: 9:30 a.m.–4:00 p.m., Mon–Fri;
1:00 p.m.–4:00 p.m., Sun.

FEES
Adults $5, seniors $3, students (with ID) $2, children under 12 free.

INFORMATION
652-8977.

DIRECTIONS
Take Highway 10 (Eastern Townships Autoroute) to Highway 30. Follow Highway 30 north (towards Sorel) to exit 128. Follow the blue panel signs to the Électrium.

Winter Activities at the Centre de Conservation de la Nature Mount St Hilaire

DRIVING TIME: 45 MIN

Photo: Centre de la Nature Mont St Hilaire

From a distance, Mount St Hilaire, a mere 40 km south of Montreal, resembles the neighbouring Mount St Bruno or our own Mount Royal. Though higher and more imposing than either, it seems typical of the rounded hills that rise suddenly from the St Lawrence Valley. But looks can be deceiving, and if you take the time to get behind the façade, you're in for a real surprise. Mount St Hilaire is actually a ring of four or five peaks encircling a large, elevated, gently undulating valley. Once inside, you'll discover a large lake, forests, streams, and a landscape you would expect only farther north in the Laurentians. You'll also discover a visitor's centre and winter activities for the whole family.

For 45 years, most of the mountain was owned by Brigadier A. Hamilton Gault, who donated it to McGill University in 1958. But it was Alice Johannsen—daughter of the famous Herman "Jackrabbit" Johannsen—who founded the nature centre and created the park. While half the mountain is set aside for research, the other half is given over to public use.

More than 100,000 visitors a year come to the nature conservation centre. Most come in autumn, when the deciduous forest lights up with colour.

But there's plenty to do in winter, too: skiing, snowshoeing, skating, tobogganing, and hiking.

At the visitor's centre, you can pick up a trail map, rent snowshoes or skis, and take a peek at a 3D replica of the mountain and trails. (Novice snowshoers take note: Straps on the snowshoes are rubber, making them very easy to put on and use.) In winter, a fireplace is kept blazing, and picnic tables are set up in the centre's exhibition hall, transforming it into a skiers' lounge.

The centre has around 20 km of trails in all, groomed by snowmobile for hiking, snowshoeing, and cross-country skiing. Some trails, are shared, but many are reserved for a single purpose. There are 8 km of ski trails, classed easy, difficult, and very difficult. Bird feeders are placed along many of them, and one trail has a heated shack.

Two trails, totalling 5.5 km, are specifically maintained for snowshoeing and hiking. Burned Hill follows the ridge along the outer edge of the mountain. It has several nice views, but offers little shelter from prevailing winds and can be rough going on cold days. Pain de Sucre (Sugarloaf), on the other hand, sticks to the inside of the valley. It starts off very gently, through a tall deciduous forest and past open brooks, but steepens quickly as it rises towards the highest of the five peaks (400 m).

The final ascent on Burned Hill is very challenging, and a pair of ski poles will really help out. Though the peak doesn't reveal itself until the last minute, when it does, it presents a spectacular panorama: the town of Mont St Hilaire, apple orchards, the Richelieu River, and, on clear days, Montreal. You'll feel as if you are high in the mountains. The trees are twisted and stunted, and are often covered in frost, so they look like a white coral garden.

Lake Hertel, a large lake in the valley, is the focus for two activities. By mid-January, the ice is generally thick enough for skating and a track is cleared along its edge. Children will enjoy tobogganing down the short snow slide and onto the ice. (Bring your own toboggan.)

SEASON AND HOURS
8 a.m.–1 hour before sunset, every day.

FEES
Adults $4, youth 6–17 and seniors $2, under 6 free.

INFORMATION
(514) 467-1755.

DIRECTIONS
Take the Champlain Bridge (staying in the right lane) and follow Highway 20 east towards Quebec City. Just across the Richelieu River, take exit 113 and follow the signs from there.

Fort Chambly
and Fort Lennox
National Historic Sites
Richelieu River

DRIVING TIME: 20 & 45 MIN

Strategically located at the foot of the rapids in Chambly is the castle-like **Fort Chambly**. Built in the French medieval style, it is an immense square grey granite structure with large bastions at each corner. Since a tour of the fort needn't take you outdoors, this is a good visit for a rainy day—though the wooded grounds on the edge of the Richelieu River are certainly pleasant in the sunshine.

Four forts have occupied the site since French colonists settled here. The first, made of wood, was built in 1665 by Jacques de Chambly to protect the colonies during the French-Iroquois wars. The French reached final and lasting peace with the Iroquois in 1701, just in time for war with the British. The current fort dates from 1709.

Regular exhibits include mannequins in regimental gear, but you may notice these soldiers are a little short. Due to a mix-up stemming from the difference between old French and modern Imperial measure, the costumers made the uniforms to fit a man of 5' 1" (1.37 m)—instead of 5' 5" (1.46 m). small mannequins were also made.

MONTÉRÉGIE

Other permanent exhibits discuss the enemies the fort was built to defend against and the difficult life of the early colonists, who were nearly wiped out by the Iroquois until Chambly's famed Carignan-Salières regiment arrived. Travelling exhibits that change yearly take a closer look at life in the New World.

If the lot of the French colonists in Chambly was difficult, that of the British soldiers at **Fort Lennox** to the south was no easier. They slept two per bed and were locked in at night to prevent desertion. The workday was long, the pay poor, and the hygiene appalling: the men washed their faces once a day—in basins used for toilets at night—their feet once a week, and the rest of their bodies a few times a year. Skin afflictions and eye diseases were common.

But you could visit Fort Lennox on Île aux Noix (Nut Island) for years without hearing the story of the fort—the setting is so beautiful, you might not want to spend time indoors. You get to the island by passenger ferry, and the half dozen granite buildings of the fort are surrounded by a moat in the shape of a five-pointed star. Kids will love this fairy-tale moat, with lily pads, duckweed, turtles, and more frogs than you can shake a blunderbuss at.

Outside the fortifications, you can picnic in the shade of a few gigantic trees or play with Frisbees, footballs, soccer balls, and other games available in the canteen—which also has light snacks and delicious home-made pastries, not to mention frozen treats.

Fort Chambly
SEASON AND HOURS
Mid-May–Jun 23:
9:00 a.m.–5:00 p.m., every day.
Jun 24–Labour Day: 10:00 a.m.–6:00 p.m., every day (except Mon).
Sept 5–Sept 30: 10:00 a.m.–5:00 p.m., every day (except Mon).
Oct 1–Dec 10: 10:00 a.m.–5:00 p.m., Wed–Sun. Tours on request.
FEES
Adults $3.25, students $1.50, under 6 free.
INFORMATION
(514) 658-1585.
DIRECTIONS
Take Highway 10 (Eastern Townships Autoroute) to exit 22 and immediately follow signs to Chambly.

Fort Lennox
SEASON AND HOURS
mid-May–mid-Oct: 10:00 a.m.–6:00 p.m., every day.
English tours at 11, 2, and 4 p.m.;
French tours at 10, 1, 3, and 5 p.m.
FEES
Adults $3, children $2.
INFORMATION
(514) 291-5700.
DIRECTIONS
Take Highway 10 (Eastern Townships Autoroute) to exit 22. Follow Highway 35 south to St Jean sur Richelieu. At Iberville take Route 223 south to St Paul de l'Île aux Noix.

George H. Montgomery
Bird Sanctuary
Philipsburg
DRIVING TIME: 50 MIN

If you've ever driven to Vermont, you've probably passed through the Philipsburg Migratory Bird Sanctuary without even knowing it. The sanctuary stretches from the village of Philipsburg to the Vermont border, from Missisquoi Bay on Lake Champlain to St Armand Rd, and straddles Route 133. While it is privately owned, visitors are welcome to stroll the wonderful trails in this 485-ha sanctuary. It is widely known for its astonishing variety of habitats and landscapes, which attract a large number of bird species, especially during the spring and fall migrations.

The sanctuary was established in 1955, and operates under the joint stewardship of several groups, including the Montgomery family and the Province of Quebec Society for the Protection of Birds (PQSPB), which maintains the network of trails. The trails are poorly marked, so it's easy to get lost, but don't worry. You can always orient yourself by the sounds of the highway. Just don't try leaving a

Photo: Cynthia Chalk

MONTÉRÉGIE

trail of bread crumbs!

The best birding, walking, and picknicking is in the vee formed by Route 133 and St Armand Rd, where a number of trails lead through various habitats, including a forest of slender maples and tall beech.

One trail follows the damp shores of Steit's Pond, a large body of water with transitional swamp and marshy areas. The pond is popular with ducks in spring and fall, and there are duck blinds on the west side of the pond, but you'll need rubber boots to hike comfortably here.

Another trail runs through the woods, then up a ridge on the pond's southeast side. It follows a cliff in a number of places and offers bird's-eye views of the pond, the highway, and Lake Champlain. When the trail leaves the cliff, it descends into a deep ravine bursting with ferns, forest wildflowers, and moss-covered rocky outcroppings. It is a different world in the ravine, under an incredibly dense canopy reminiscent of the rain forest path to Wreck Beach in Vancouver.

Just east of the pond and over a low fence is a huge field with a view of rolling farmland, cornfields, and the Adirondacks to the south that looks like a painting by an old master. The field adjoins, but is not part of, the sanctuary. Under the huge tree in the centre of the field is a great place for a picnic. The owner, Mr. Audette, has provided some picnic tables, and has placed half a dozen old-fashioned bathtubs side by side in a small creek that flows through his land. He keeps them clean of moss and algae, and invites you to have a soak in the cold running water. Now there's a photo!

SEASON AND HOURS
Sunrise to sunset, every day, all year.

FEES
Free.

INFORMATION
PQSPB (514) 637-2141.

DIRECTIONS
Take the Champlain Bridge and follow Highway 10 (Eastern Townships Autoroute) east to exit 22. Follow Highway 35 south to Iberville, where it joins Route 133. Continue south on Route 133 to Philipsburg.
At Philipsburg, you can continue to the Motel de la Frontière, on the east side of the highway, where you can park for free, as long as you ask the owners' permission. Parking is also free in the Montgomery's field, but you have to turn left across the highway onto St Armand Rd. Just beyond the Montgomery's field you can park for $2 in Mr. Audette's parking lot and enter the sanctuary through his land. You can't miss the white pebbled entrance and large sign.

Coeur du Québec

Though it is also known as Mauricie–Bois Franc, the region's tourism name of Coeur du Québec (Quebec Heartland) seems to suit it better. South of the St Lawrence its geography is quite typical of the flat, mainly agricultural St Lawrence Lowlands— but north of the river, it becomes wilder where it quite suddenly meets the southern limits of the Canadian Shield. Outside the main cities and towns, the sparsely populated region is marked by rocky outcroppings, dense forests, winding roads, and charming villages untouched by time.

This is the setting for two of the province's largest rural gatherings. Every spring, *hundreds of thousands of snow geese stop over for a few weeks in the flooded fields of Baie du Febvre. Their daily departure at dawn and return at dusk is one of the most fantastic sights in the province.* In the fall, the small town of St Tite, north of Trois Rivières, welcomes hundreds of thousands of visitors to its annual rodeo and western festival—the largest of its kind in eastern Canada.

If you'd rather stay away from crowds, the park at St Ursule is a better destination. At any time of year, you'll find one of the nicest waterfalls within easy reach of Montreal.

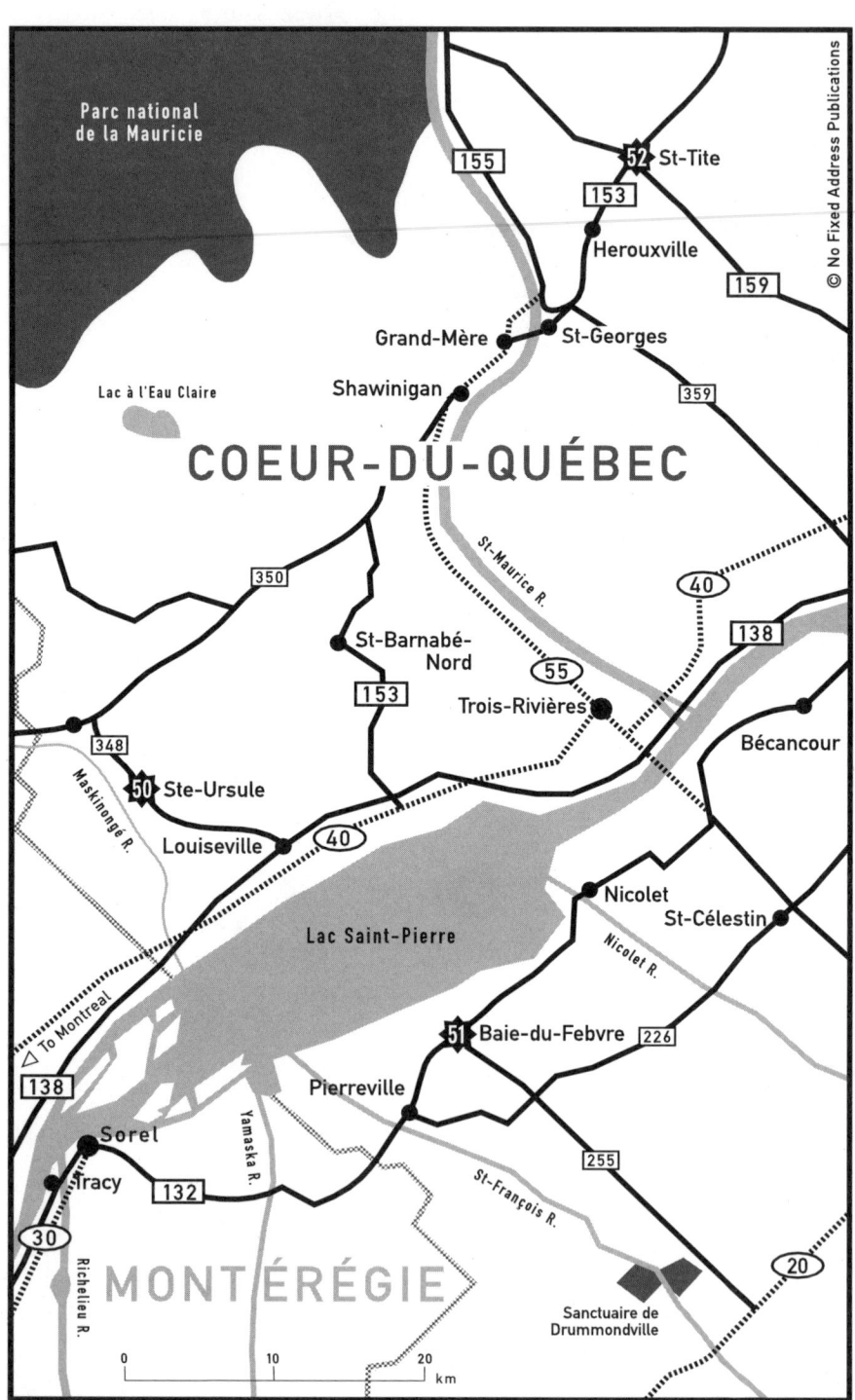

COEUR DU QUÉBEC

Trip Destinations

🔷50 Parc des Chutes St Ursule
(Waterfalls)
St Ursule
(819) 228-3555
p.134

🔷51 Snow Geese Staging Grounds
Baie du Febvre
(514) 783-6996 (seasonal)
p.136

🔷52 St Tite Western Festival
St Tite
(418) 365-7524 (seasonal)
p.138

Tourist Information

Mauricie–Bois Francs Tourist
Association
(819) 375-1222, (800) 567-7603

Waterfalls at
Parc des Chutes
St Ursule
DRIVING TIME: 1 HR

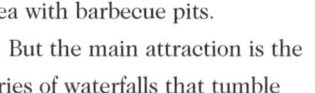

The thundering waterfalls at St Ursule, one of the best-kept secrets of the region, make an exciting day-trip destination. Created by an earthquake in 1663, the falls were the site of one of Quebec's first pulp mills. Today, they are managed by a non-profit organization that leases the land from Hydro-Québec, which reserves the right to future development.

Nature walks through the dense woods are always pleasant, and the park offers a variety of seasonal workshops. There is a fast-food restaurant in the visitor's centre, a playground, and a picnic area with barbecue pits.

But the main attraction is the series of waterfalls that tumble through the park. From its source in the lake of the same name, the Maskinongé River runs nearly straight to the St Lawrence—until it reaches the park. Here, the river plunges five times, foaming madly, for a total vertical spill of over 71 m.

For a self-guided tour of the falls, pick up a pamphlet (French only) at the visitor's centre. If you're feeling a little adventurous, you can walk the hilly

134   Get Outta Town!

footpath on the island formed when the river changed course. (The old bed is high and dry except during the spring run-off.) Otherwise do as most of the 45,000 annual visitors do, and stroll along the park's well-maintained boardwalks, from the top of the falls to the bottom. No matter which path you take, the sound of the falls and the sweet smells of the lush woods will follow you every step.

The first and second waterfalls are wide and graceful, flowing alongside a spectacular railway trestle bridge.

The third is a scant 100 m away, where the river changed direction as a result of the quake. If turbulence is the measure of a waterfall's beauty, this is by far the most splendid, roaring a couple of hundred metres down a deep, narrow gorge. Flanked by almost vertical cliffs topped with tall spruce, its 45-degree descent creates a mesmerizing torrent of white water and standing waves.

Not far along the boardwalk is the belvedere. This enormous wooden lookout tower stands 16 m on the side of a ridge. It is worth the 81-step climb for the picture-postcard view of the falls directly below, the 45-degree falls upriver, and the surrounding countryside. A couple of picnic tables under a covered shelter make the belvedere a great place for a picnic lunch, rain or shine.

Spray drifts off the final falls and across the lower part of the final observation platform, a short walk down the ridge from the belvedere.

For geologists, the area at the bottom of the falls is a textbook study. The falls were formed on a fault line that runs from Joliette to Shawinigan. At two places—near the bottom of the island and around the bend—the fault is clearly visible. Also, the falls cleave the earth precisely where the granite-like gneiss of the Canadian Shield meets the sedimentary rock of the St Lawrence Lowland.

SEASON AND HOURS
All year.
Visitor's centre and restrooms: Apr–Oct, every day; weekends only from Labour Day to St Jean Baptiste Day (June 24).

FEES
Adults $3.50, seniors, $2.50, youth 10-18 $2.00, children 5–10 $1.00, children under 5 free. Group rates.

INFORMATION
(819) 228-3555. Tours in English with advance notice.

DIRECTIONS
Take Highway 40 east to exit 166. From there, follow Route 138 east to Louiseville, then head north on Route 348 through St Ursule. Beyond St Ursule, follow the clearly marked signs to the Parc des Chutes de Sainte Ursule.

Snow Geese
Staging Grounds
Baie du Febvre

DRIVING TIME: 1 HR 40 MIN

Twice a year, hundreds of thousands of snow geese migrate 8,000 km between their wintering grounds down south and their breeding grounds in the Arctic. In autumn, the geese travel south at varying times, stopping at several places, though mainly in the Quebec City area. In spring, however, the geese all leave together and stop only once, in a few flooded fields in the town of Baie du Febvre. These graceful geese are huge, beautiful, snow white, and noisy. The sight and sound of huge rafts of them taking off at dawn or settling at dusk is unforgettable.

Lake St Pierre, the halfway point in their journey, normally has an area of 250 km², but when the St Lawrence swells with the spring thaw it floods, covering an area almost double in size. This is ideal for the geese, which like to overnight in shallow water, so they can hear the approach of predators. Another attraction is all the corn and other grain left in nearby fields from the previous autumn's harvest.

Despite these favourable conditions, the geese were once on the verge of extinction. Intensive farming methods included the draining of flooded fields, which put pressure on the population. In the '70s, Ducks Unlimited convinced the local people of the potential for tourism and built dikes to control the flooding. Now, fields are kept flooded during the migration period and aren't drained until early May, still leaving plenty of time for planting.

The program has been a quacking success. In 1970, 300 snow geese stopped off at Baie du Febvre, but it is estimated that last year, 300,000 snow geese, 70,000 Canada geese, and 15,000 ducks of various species congregated there for up to three weeks.

During the day, there is little to see at Baie du Febvre, since the geese are feeding in fields up to 50 km away. The real shows are at dawn and dusk, when the waterfowl flock to and from the flooded fields on the edge of town.

The visitor's centre, an attractive two-storey red brick building, is located on the edge of Route 132, just across from the most popular field. Here, you can pick up a map showing the four viewing areas and a pamphlet listing goose-related events in town, including an annual art exhibition. The centre has a small museum, with displays and panels (in French only) explaining the migration and the flooding and listing the species that visit the area. You can rent binoculars, or take a gander at the fields from the upper deck, where binoculars are installed.

But the best experience is to be had out on the edge of the fields. About 40 min before sunset, the flocks begin returning. Soon the sky is filled with endless streams of geese, like bees around a busy hive. This continues at full tilt for half an hour, with the geese circling and landing in a big flurry of feathers. The honking is marvellous, and with a good pair of binoculars you'll be able to see the geese grooming at the water's edge, looking very much like huge clumps of snow against the muddy fields. Apparently, sunrise can be even more spectacular, since the geese rise into the air *en masse*.

The visitor's centre is wheelchair accessible.

SEASON AND HOURS
Snow geese: Early to mid–April
Canada geese: Early April until the end of the month.
FEES
Visitor's centre: Adults $3, under 12 free.
INFORMATION
(514) 783-6996 (seasonal).
DIRECTIONS
Go over the Champlain Bridge and take Highway 10 (Eastern Townships Autoroute) to exit 11 (Sorel–Québec). Follow Highway 30 north to Sorel, then join Route 132 east to Baie du Febvre. The visitor's centre is on Route 132.

52

Western Festival
St Tite
DRIVING TIME: 2 HR

As summer draws to a close, polish up your Tony Lamas and shine your spurs, 'cause Quebec goes Western. For 10 days each September, the quiet little town of St Tite (pop. 4,000) welcomes 350,000 visitors to a full-blown rodeo, the largest in eastern Canada. Over 300 professional cowboys and cowgirls from Canada and the U.S. compete for $130,000 in prize money. On weekends you'll see prime steer wrestling (*terrassement de bouvillon*), steer roping (*prise de veau au lasso*), and rodeo clowns (*clowns de taureau*).

But this is more than just a rodeo: it is a unique cultural experience. Up to a week before the festival begins, visitors start rolling in to stake their claims. Local merchants lease their storefronts to vendors, and residents rent out their backyards to visitors. By the time the rodeo is underway, nearly every inch of available space is taken up by vendors, hawkers, and food stalls, not to mention tents, trailers, and motor homes.

The whole town pitches in to make this the friendliest, most welcoming Western crowd east of the Bow River. Parts of town are permanently gussied up in Western motifs—street signs are in a Western style, for example—and just about everyone decorates their lawns with bales of hay and other cowpoke accoutrements.

The opening parade is an annual highlight held the first Sunday of the festival at 1 p.m. The parade features animal-drawn floats, buggies, and covered wagons—almost 300 entries in all. There is a very special feeling as it winds its way merrily along the narrow streets lined with prosperous-looking clapboard houses and up to a 100,000 people. Youth groups and marching bands practise all year for this event, and many of the spectators know someone in the parade.

The two shopping streets are absolutely crammed with vendors and crowds. There's no shortage of pizza, steamed hot-dogs, or the popular French fries with cheese curd and gravy known as *poutine*. You'll find slightly more upscale fast food in an outdoor food court nearer the rodeo grounds, and you can't go wrong with corn on the cob, served everywhere water can be boiled.

There are four professional rodeo days during the festival. The two days of the opening weekend offer good value for money, while the finales on the last weekend showcase top-notch performances, which are generally sold out well ahead of time. If you're new to the rodeo scene, you'll enjoy either weekend. I got a big kick out of the cowboys on speeding horses who traded places, and some bucking bull-riding. While the rock n' roll blaring throughout the events was a bit trying, at half-time intermission it was amazing to see the entire crowd dancing to the Village People's "YMCA," led by the rodeo clowns and cowboys.

In comparison, the much-touted Artisan Village and Children's Village are somewhat disappointing. The Artisan Village consists of a couple of Western-looking stalls selling the same products available elsewhere in town. The Children's Village is not much more than a sandbox and the usual playground equipment. But the general ambience in the streets more than makes up for the few letdowns, and in rainy weather a number of tents provide shelter and indoor entertainment.

SEASON AND HOURS
Sept 5–14 (1997).
FEES
First weekend: Adults $12, children 2–12 $5; Second Saturday: Adults $16; Grand Finale (Sunday) $17; Parking: approximately $5.
INFORMATION
(418) 365-7524;
Reservations: (418) 365-6366.
DIRECTIONS
Highway 40 east to exit 196 (Trois Rivières). From there, take Highway 55 (Trans-Québecoise) north past Shawinigan and Grand-Mère. From St Georges, follow Route 153 east to St Tite.

Index

Note that page numbers refer to the first page of the article of interest.

A
arts and crafts
    1001 Pots, 32
    Lake Memphremagog Art Tour, 76
autumn leaves
    Centre Touristique et Éducatif des Laurentides, 36
    Morgan Arboretum, 84
    Mont St Hilaire, 124

B
Baie du Febvre, 136
Bedford, 66
beaches
    Lac Simon, 16
    Lac des Plages, 16
    Le Sablon, 48
    Rawdon, 48
    Rawdon Rapids, 48
    St Zotique, 16
bees
    Hydromelerie Intermiel, 116
bicycling
    see cycling
    see also mountain biking
birdwatching
    Baie du Febvre, 136
    Cooper Marsh Conservation Area, 104
    George H. Montgomery Bird Sanctuary, 128
    see also nature centres
Bois de l'Île Bizard Nature Centre, 88
Bois de Liesse Nature Centre, 88
Bonsecours Basin, 92
Brome County Fair, 70
Brome County Historical Society Museum, 72

C
Canadian Railway Museum, 96
canoeing
    Centre Touristique et Éducatif des Laurentides, 36
    Parc des Amoureux, 30
Cantons de l'Est *see Eastern Townships*
Cap St Jacques Nature Centre, 88

Cèdres, 114
Centre de la Nature Laval *see Laval Nature Centre*
Centre Touristique et Éducatif des Laurentides, 36
Centre Plein Air Les Forestiers, 114
Chambly, 126
Chutes Peine à Monter et Dalles, 56
Coeur du Québec, 130–138
Cooper Marsh Conservation Area, 104
Cosmodome, 90
Coteau du Lac National Historic Site, 110
cross-country skiing
    Cap St Jacques Nature Centre, 88
    Laval Nature Centre, 92
    Doncaster Park, 28
    Gatineau Park, 20
    Hôtel l'Estérel, 34
    Mont St Hilaire, 124
    Morgan Arboretum 84

county fairs *see fairs*
cycling
    Bois de l'Île Bizard, 88
    Bois de Liesse, 88
    Cap St Jacques, 88
    Doncaster Park, 28
    Île de la Visitation, 94
    Montagne Coupée, 52
    Pointe aux Prairies, 94
    see also mountain biking

D
deer
    Duhamel, 14
    Ecomuseum, 86
    Omega Domaine, 12
Delson
dogs (parks where permitted)
    Gatineau Park, 20
    Île de la Visitation Nature Park, 94
    Doncaster Park, 28
dogsledding
    Centre Plein Air Les Forestiers, 114
    Hôtel l'Estérel, 34
    Laval Nature Centre, 92
    Doncaster Park, 28
Dorwin Falls, 46

140 Get Outta Town!

Dunham, 66
Duhamel
   deer observation, 14
   Lac Simon beach, 16

E
Earle Moore's Canadiana Village, 50
Eastern Townships, 60-76
Ecomuseum, 86
Électrium, 122
Estérel, 34
Estrie see *Eastern Townships*
Exotarium, 118

F
fairs
   Brome County Fair, 70
   Jovi-Foire (summertime fair), 38
farms
   Cap St Jacques, 88
   Llamadu, 68
Fête Nationale see *St Jean Baptiste Day*
flower gardens
   Val David 30
forts
   Chambly, 126
   Coteau du Lac, 110
   Lennox, 126

G
Gatineau Park, 20
George H. Montgomery Bird Sanctuary, 128
gliding see *soaring*
Gregorian chanting, 74

H
Hawkesbury, 18
hiking
   Centre Touristique et Éducatif des Laurentides, 36
   Doncaster Park, 28
   Gatineau Park, 20
   Mont Tremblant Provincial Park, 40
   Parc Régional des Sept Chutes, 58
historic sites
   Coteau du Lac, 110
   Earl Moore's Canadiana Village, 50
   Fort Chambly, 126
   Fort Lennox, 126
   Pointe du Buisson Archaeological Site, 120

Pointe du Moulin, 82
horseback riding
   Montagne Coupée, 52
   St Tite Western Festival, 138
hot-air ballooning
   Hôtel l'Estérel, 34
Hôtel l'Estérel, 34
Hydromelerie Intermiel, 116

I
ice-skating
   Bonsecours Basin, 92
   Centre Plein Air Les Forestiers, 114
   Hôtel l'Estérel, 34
   Laval Nature Centre, 92
   Mont St Hilaire, 124
   Île de la Visitation Nature Park, 94
in-line skating
   Montagne Coupée, 52
Indian culture
   Kahnawake Powwow, 112
   Kanesatake Powwow, 112
   Pointe du Buisson Archaeological Site, 120
inner-tubing see *tobogganing*
   see also *waterslides*

J
Jovi-Foire (summertime fair), 38

K
Kahnawake, 112
Kanesatake, 112
·kicksledding
   Centre Plein Air Les Forestiers, 114
   Gatineau Park, 20
   Montagne Coupée, 52

L
Lanaudière, 42–58
Laurentians, 22–40
Laurentides see *Laurentians*
Laval see *Montreal, Laval, and South Shore*
Laval Nature Centre, 92
Llamadu, 68
llamas, 68
luge finlandaise see *kicksledding*

M
maps
   Coeur du Québec, 132
   Eastern Townships, 62

Lanaudière, 44
Laurentians, 24
Montérégie, 102
Montreal, Laval, and South Shore, 80
Outaouais, 10
marshes
    Bois de l'Île Bizard Nature Park, 88
    Cooper Marsh Conservation Area, 104
    Pointe aux Prairies Nature Park, 94
    Marsil Museum of Clothing, Textiles, and Fibre, 98
Mauricie–Bois Francs see *Coeur du Québec*
Memphremagog Art Tour, 76
Missisquoi Historical Society Museum, 64
Mont Rolland, 28
Mont Tremblant Provincial Park, 40
Montagne Coupée, 52
Montebello, 16
Montérégie, 100–128
Montreal, Laval, and South Shore, 78–96
Morgan Arboretum, 84
mountain biking
    Montagne Coupée, 52
    Mont Tremblant, 40
    see also cycling
MUC Nature Centres
    see nature centres
museums
    Brome County Historical Society Museum, 72
    Earle Moore's Canadiana Village, 50
    Louis Cyr Museum, 54
    Marsil Museum of Clothing, Textiles, and Fibre, 64
    Missisquoi Historical Society Museum, 64
    Pointe du Buisson Archaeological Site, 120
    see also historic sites
    see also science centres
music
    Gregorian chanting, 74
    Jovi-Foire (summertime fair), 38

N
nature centres
    Bois de l'Île Bizard, 88
    Bois de Liesse, 88
    Cap St Jacques, 88
    Île de la Visitation, 94

Laval, 92
Pointe aux Prairies, 94
see also parks

O
1001 Pots, 32
Oka 112, 116
Omega Domaine, 12
Outaouais, 8–20

P
parks
    Chutes Peine a Monter et Dalles, 56
    Chutes de St Ursule, 134
    Doncaster, 28
    Gatineau, 20
    Laval Nature Centre, 92
    Morgan Arboretum, 84
    Parc des Amoureux, 30
    Pointe du Moulin, 82
    Rivière du Nord (Wilson Falls), 26
    Sept Chutes, 58
    see also nature centres
Pointe du Buisson Archaeological Site, 120
Pointe du Moulin, 82
powwows
    Kahnawake, 112
    Kanesatake, 112
    see also Indian culture

R
Rawdon
    Dorwin Falls 46
    Earle Moore's Canadiana Village, 50
    municipal beach, 48
    Rawdon Rapids, 48
Rigaud, 108
Rivière du Nord Regional Park (Wilson Falls), 26
recreation centres
    Montagne Coupée, 52
    Centre Plein Air Les Forestiers, 114
reptiles, 118
road maps
    see maps
rodeos
    St Tite 138
roller-blading
    see in-line skating

S

St Agathe, 36
St Benoît du Lac monastery, 74
St Constant, 96
St Faustin, 36
St Hilaire, 124
St Jean Baptiste Day, 92
St Jean de Matha, 54
St Jérôme, 26
St Jovite, 38
St Lambert, 98
St Paul de l'Île aux Noix, 126
St Polycarpe, 106
St Télésphore, 106
St Tite, 138
St Ursule, 134
St Zotique, 106
science centres
    Cosmodome, 90
    Électrium, 122
Sept Chutes Regional Park, 58
skating
    see ice-skating
skiing see cross-country skiing
snowmobiling
    Outaouais, 14
    Laurentians, 34
snowshoeing
    Gatineau Par,k 20
    Mont St Hilaire, 124
snow geese, 136
South Shore see *Montreal, Laval, and South Shore*
Stanbridge East, 64
Sucrerie de la Montagne, 108
sugaring off
    Sucrerie de la Montagne, 108
    Owl Hoot Maple Farm, 64
swimming see *beaches*

T

tobogganing
    Duhamel, 14
    Centre Plein Air Les Forestiers, 114
    Laval Nature Centre, 92
    Mont St Hilaire, 124

tours
    art, 76
    wine, 66
trains
    Canadian Railway Museum, 96

V

Val David
    1001 Pots, 32
    Park des Amoureux, 30
    rock garden, 30
    P'tit Train du Nord (bike path), 30
vineyards, 66

W

walking see *hiking*
waterfalls
    Chutes Peine à Monter et Dalles, 56
    Dorwin Falls, 46
    Rawdon Rapids, 48
    Rivière du Nord Park (Wilson Falls), 26
    Sept Chutes (Seven Falls), 58
    St Ursule, 134
waterslides
    Le Sablon, 106
wildlife observation see *birdwatching, deer, snow geese, wildlife parks*
wildlife parks
    Ecomuseum, 86
    Omega Domaine, 12
    Llamadu, 68
    see also *farms, zoos*
windmills
    Pointe du Moulin, 82
workshops
    1001 Pots, 32
    Lake Memphremagog Art Tour, 76

Z

zoos
    Ecomuseum, 86
    Exotarium, 118
    Laval Nature Centre, 92
    Omega Domaine, 12
    see also *farms, wildlife parks*

Comments—Suggestions

Prices go up, places change ownership, and festivals change dates. What was terrific one time of year might be disappointing at another. Sometimes errors simply find their way into the text. Or maybe you have a secret destination you'd like to share with other readers. Whatever the reason, we'd love to hear from you, so don't hesitate to send us your comments or suggestions for improvements.

Write to:
No Fixed Address Publications
P.O. Box 65, NDG Station
Montreal, Quebec
H4A 3P4
Canada

e-mail: nfa@cam.org

Ordering a Copy

If you enjoyed Get Outta Town! Montreal and would like to order a copy directly from the publisher, simply fill out the form below (or a photocopy of it). Travel agents, educators, and tour guides, please inquire for volume discounts.

Title	Quantity	Price	Total
Get Outta Town! Montreal	_____	$14.95	_____
Escapades d'un jour, Montréal	_____	$14.95	_____
		Sub-total	_____
		GST in Canada 7% ($1.05 per book)	
		Total (includes shipping and handling)	_____

Name: _____ Address: _____

City: _____ Postal Code: _____

Payment: ☐ Money Order   ☐ Visa   ☐ Mastercard   ☐ Cheque

Card Number: _____ Expiry Date: _____

Signature: _____